THE REVELATOR

A NOVEL

ROBERT KLOSS

The Unnamed Press
Los Angeles, CA

The Unnamed Press
1551 Colorado Blvd., Suite #201
Los Angeles, CA 90041
www.unnamedpress.com

Published in North America by The Unnamed Press.

1 3 5 7 10 8 6 4 2

ISBN: 978-1-939419-50-7

Library of Congress Control Number: 2015945877

This book is distributed by Publishers Group West
Printed in the United States of America by McNaughton & Gunn

Designed by Scott Arany
Cover design by Jaya Nicely
Cover illustration by Matt Kish

To Karissa

THE REVELATOR

I had a dream,
which was not all a dream.
—LORD BYRON,
"DARKNESS"

Death is a house inside the forest.
Come. I am made of many doors.
—CLAIRE HERO,
"THE NIGHT WAS ANIMAL"

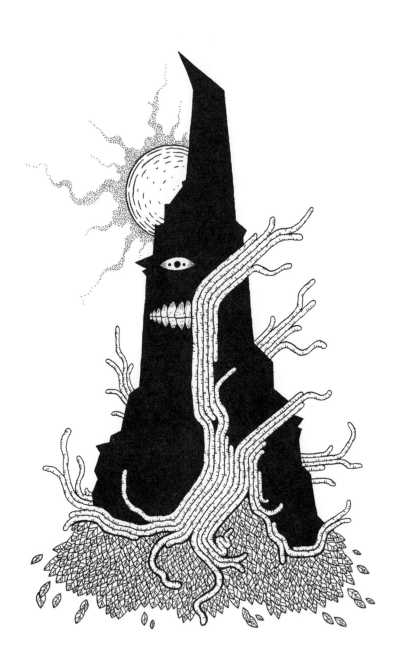

PROLOGUE
THE
DAYS
OF MAN

They drifted for months aboard a ship they called the *Spotted One*, locked between the vast, merciless blue and the withering sun. Their faces blistered and their minds bleached and weary. They conspired in the shadows, drew plans in the sawdust. They grew confident and foolhardy. Finally, the Admiral consulted his god and ordered them shot through the skulls, their bodies weighted with lead and dropped to the depths, with neither forgiveness nor prayer.

And the sun swelled red, and the sky shimmered, and the gulls swirled, screaming. Soon the black mountain jutted from the horizon. And some considered it a mirage, and some named it the "Finger of the Evil One," and some called it a tower of soot, dreamed it an ancient citadel misshapen by flame, the horror of all trapped within. The Admiral alone crossed himself and raised his book to the winds, saying, "Father, I see you now."

For the sun's unrelenting sheen, the men remained below-decks, ladling their chests with green water. The games they played with dice, with lice, these men in the shadows, nude but for their leggings, their laughter as they gnawed salt pork. Ever echoing upon the deck, the Admiral's leaden pacing as he regarded the nearing shore, calling the Almighty's name, and those names he gave the black mountain ever upon the horizon.

Each day ever as the days before, until the exhilarated call of the lookout announced the vast wilderness before them. And the Admiral with all the maps and books of his knowledge, their descriptions of the Orient, its towers and merchants and treasures, turned to his crew and said, "By morning we will be dressed in silks. We will smell of spices and our bodies will glisten with oil." Now fires lit the evening shores, and the night was born into heathen drums, screams and whoops, and within this cacophony the Admiral announced, "Sleep with your muskets readied."

Soon the natives ventured forth, bodies painted blue or black or red, bones impaling their noses, their brows, their cheeks. How the lines of their canoes drifted the waters. How the dawn sheened with their arrows aflame. The Admiral and his crew waited in armor with horsehair plumes, their swords and muskets readied, and when he commanded, the explosion of musket fire, the acrid punch of gun smoke. And natives leapt from their canoes and natives sloshed in blood, while gulls investigated the cooling bodies, consumed the eyes, the cheeks, and soon the bloated and rotting rest.

The crew went ashore firing muskets, the red sun tinting their armor until they seemed born in the fires of another world. And the natives fled into the forests while others fell to their knees, the whites of their eyes and teeth outlandish against their bodies rubbed black with soot. The crew took these stragglers by the clumps of their hair, held them down, bound their wrists and ankles with rope, and before these hostages they waited, until at last those who had fled slowly returned. And they returned suppliant, pressed their brows to the sand and offered the smoked meat of many colored birds, and fruits, orange and hideously spiked, their yellow flesh dripping with sweetness. They called the Admiral and his crew a word the Admiral translated for the others as "gods." He said, "They call us 'lords from the sky.'" He said, "I have gestured across the waters, and they believe we have come from the heavens." And when the Admiral indicated the black mountain, asked of its genesis, its distance from where they stood, the natives gazed at him as if he were mad, as if he were pointing at nothing at all.

To follow were days of bounty. While the Admiral trekked the lands, his crew lounged in beds of rope strung between palms, and now the ladies of the island cooled them with the waving of palm fronds. "What lovelies are these," wrote one sailor, "voluptuous and wild and totally submissive to the whims of man." And in the nights they feasted on smoked birds and barbecued lizards, and when the broken open skull of a monkey was offered none of the crew resisted scooping the brain. And in the nights they drank of a fermented root brew, each man singing and dancing in the manner of his civilization, calling out the songs and melodies of his home. In the firelight all men were as brothers before one another and all men were as husbands unto the women. And many coupled without struggle and with great pleasure on the sands of the beach, the surf licking their feet. How they lay together, breathless and silent, having already spoken the only language they held mutual.

Alone on his vessel rocking with the surf, the Admiral wrote by candle flame, "Perhaps we have not arrived at the Orient. So much of the innocence of the people—their unashamed nakedness, their inability to comprehend guile and vanity and greed—indeed, so much of this world, the beauty and splendor and plenty—hints at some far deeper significance," and later he wrote, "I have sometimes wondered if we are not at the threshold of Paradise."

At midday next the chief returned from the forest, with feathers ragged, and blackened face streaked by tears. His people watched as he wept and beat the ground before the Admiral. Their anguished silence as he reached to his captors, and whispered a word the Admiral translated as "brother." Now the Admiral took the chief's jangling bracelets in hand. "This metal," the Admiral asked, "there is more?"

And in his journal the Admiral wrote, "I have wondered, Father, what is your purpose in leading me here? Perhaps I now understand."

Now the natives foraged for gold at their chief's commandment, their shadows silent in the forests, their muddy figures sifting near the rivers. Those who brought nuggets were rewarded with pretty glass and tin bells, and those who returned with nothing were thrashed. A man's face as he bellows in the dirt, coughing blood. A man's eyes as his wife watches him from the door of their hut, as his son observes from behind his mother, as he is spat upon. In the days to follow these men were discovered slouched against trees, their jugulars sliced with spear tips, their life drained to the soil.

And in the early days of these labors the natives were allowed to freely move about their camps, for if one man fled his friend would be shot, or his wife and children would be slaughtered. And the Admiral addressed those who worked the hardest, saying, "You will make wondrous workers back home." He clapped them on the back and he gave them bells, while in his journal he wrote, "The king will be pleased to learn these heathens are quick to labor and vigorous in their duties."

And while the native men sought the forests for gold, the Admiral's men gathered the comeliest of the native women—their round hips and bare, ample breasts—and brought them to the ship. And when the women fought back, when they gouged and drew lines of blood in the sailors' backs, across their throats and faces, when they bit and tore and gnashed, they were tied down and thrashed with rope until lips were mashed and teeth spat into a bloody muck and eyes made fat and purple. "These shameless bitches," wrote one sailor by candlelight, his native woman pummeled and asleep in his bunk, "go about attired in leaves or in nothing at all, such is their lustiness, and yet they act as uninitiated as nuns when brought to our quarters. However, I can assure you, after a thrashing or two they all take to the act with such vigor and skill you would think even the youngest of them were raised in a brothel."

These women returned to their husbands hobbled and bruised faced and bite marked and impregnated, and their husbands would not look upon them. So now the beaten bodies of abandoned women lay in the mud at the farthest edge of camp. And when the children called out for their mothers they were told the women they observed in the distance were not living women, but the spirits of the dead. "Call not to them," said the fathers in their heathen tongue, "for the souls of the dead long to devour the living."

And when the chief refused the ravishing of his wives he was beaten with musket butts and accused of treason. And when the charges were read the chief wept and waved his hands, while the Admiral informed his crew, "The chief has plotted against us. He means to see us murdered in the night." So the chief was imprisoned within his hut and forbidden any interaction. And the Admiral confiscated his possessions: his casks of fermented root, his huts and feathers and spears, and his wives too were confiscated and made to lie with the crew. From the Admiral's ship they never returned, save those who washed ashore.

And while many of the crew played, the Admiral strode amidst his toiling natives, their knees sunk into the mud. The baskets of woven grass they filled with sludge and glinting nuggets. How he ordered the natives thrashed when their vigor waned. The way their faces slouched into the blood-blackened mud when they toppled, and how they wept for the world newly born about them. And when one native fled the Admiral ordered him destroyed, the natives hollering for the musket roar. And when the balls sailed harmless overhead the Admiral ordered another volley, and when this missed save for vines and tree trunks and a monkey blown out of its skin, the Admiral ordered the native tracked through the brush. He was found in the shadows, shivering, and his ankle broken. They beat him with musket butts. And when the ghost had fled they carried him through the overgrowth and tossed his corpse to the Admiral. So the Admiral ordered the native's ears removed, and these were strung yet dripping around the Admiral's neck. There they dried and shriveled. Ever outward, they listened.

And when the rivers and forests no longer offered their riches, the Admiral sent his natives to unknown depths. And when they returned with mere tufts of cotton or berries or nuts or clumps of mud, the Admiral ordered the chief's ears also removed. His screams at the cut of the blade. How these appendages dripped from their crescent around the Admiral's neck.

And the Admiral ordered the chief hanged upside down, his face purpling, the drip of his ear caverns, and soon the mad gust of flies, creeping his flesh. To the assembled natives the Admiral said, "Let this be a lesson to you all." And they did not speak or move and they could not even weep. They merely *sagged*. Now only at the show of musket fire did they slowly disperse.

And when the natives no more rose from their huts they were thrashed until they gathered their baskets and returned to the jungle. And soon they refused to rise, no matter the beating. They took their beatings limp and they no longer wept. Nor did they cover their faces when the rope lashed. Nor did they cry out. Only the dull thump of the rope against the meat of their bodies, the savage grunts of their torturer. And when they refused food, when their ribs bulged against their paling skins, when their eyes sunk into caverns, slowly now their bodies piled against huts, in the forests, on the beach. Their heartbeats imperceptible and stilling and then done. And when all the natives lay fly covered and bloating, or made the meal of the horned lizards and squawking birds, now the Admiral, his nose covered with rags, said, "The Almighty has come to me in a dream. He has said this land is not the Orient." And the Admiral gestured to the black mountain on the horizon, saying, "There is the land we seek."

So they pulled on their armor and plumes. So they readied their muskets and gathered what smoked meat and fruit and water they could heft. They stepped over putrid corpses and touched torches to the huts. From thatched roof to roof went the blue-orange of flame, and black smoke coughed and wrapped the sky. The sound such fires make, the booming and crackling of voices far older than the earliest utterances of man. Soon the native bodies gone to char save those bodies on the beach. There the crabs inspected and plundered, there the surf washed over, there the weeds tangled and the gulls did feast.

BOOK 1
HIS
BLACK
MOUNTAIN

I. Your mother lay pale and bleeding in the tangled sheets when in the flight of her soul you announced yourself wailing into the world. The women in their bonnets and housedresses crossed themselves and muttered prayers while your father called out from his sorrow. He could never again gaze upon this woman, or say her name but with a strangled sound, and he commanded her body removed. They wrapped and carried her in those very sheets, blood matted and sticky with viscera, fly gathered already, to the edge of what was considered the yard. And so with all images and possessions of this woman, carried in bedsheets and set afire. Now your father regarded you from the edge of the room, saying unto his sister, "What shall I do with this one?" And the spinster, stern and manly, said with gray lips, "I will tend after him. I will tend after the both of you." How in the brief years to follow your aunt was carried off in a fever and then your father was himself compelled to the soil, his blood misted before the plow, and into the mysterious overgrowth his hired man fled with your young stepmother. And when they found you in the dust they said you were red with the blood of your father.

II. Now this farmer in his felt hat and overcoat and this woman in her housedress and apron, her graying hair bundled, found you and gave you a bed within their barn, fed you bluing crusts and broth in the late evening, the oily clots along the surface, and they clasped your hands, bade you bless this meal with the name of the Almighty. And as you ate, the sounds and smells of those animals below, the exhilaration of barn cats and the horror of those they sought, the strand of tail dangling from maws, and elsewhere the chewing of cattle and horses and the confusion of chickens.

And when you reached for the farmer you called him "Father," and to you the farmer said, "Your father lays forgotten in the soil!" and when you reached for the farmer's wife you called her "Mother," and she leapt back, crying out, "Do you mean to curse me, child?"

When the children of the house attended school, you attended to the chores: the extracting of milk and the creation of butter and the dispersing of seeds to the dust. And in the evenings you looked to your chores while the children giggled and whispered, the blond girl with pale brows, and the two blond boys who sat shoulder to shoulder upon the steps, each clasping a half-consumed apple. And when finished the brothers tossed the cores to the dust-yard, chortling, "Give that to the pigs." So you gathered the fruit and dispensed the browning flesh, while they hooted and jeered.

The actual names of the brothers went unused, for in every aspect they seemed the same lad, save the scar along the one's cheek and the scar along the other's knuckles. And never was one boy seen without the other, for they toiled in unison: the dispersing of seed, the lugging of water from the pump, their infrequent studies before the ebbing flicker of a candle, the dubious frenzy of their quills. Yes, these boys inseparable in all doings, even in the way they stood in awe as their father slit the throat of the offering, mouths agape and hands on chubby hips, or how they went at the furtive task of throttling some chicken, giggling and panting with excitement, the breathless, agitated way they inspected the interior with fingers and penknives.

And you watched these lads through barn-wall openings, measured their ways and the ways of those they loved. And in the dust you drew a man and a woman and a girl and two brothers, watched them in what sunlight shone through. When you attempted to draw them moving they grazed in mute stupor like cattle, or milled in circles like hens, or waited, crouched, like barn cats. And you attempted to make them speak but mustered only soft moos, clucking sounds. And you now longed only for that moment when you could replicate their true motions and interactions.

And through candle-glow-tinted windows you noted the family's manner: how the father held the mother in those rich seconds when no child seemed near, and the way the daughter gazed from her bedroom window to the moonlight, silent, wistful, her elbows upon the sills, her sighs, and how the boys chased each other shouting and throwing pebbles in the day and tussled in their room in the night. The way the family prayed before their meals and thus these prayers you ever said before your own humble dinner. And you saw the father hold one lad's arm while he thrashed the other boy after they set fire to a barn cat or pelted a hog with rocks, giggling the while. And how the brothers swelled before an offering. Now the lamb's bleating, the foreboding of rank death, the burning smells. And you watched as the boys watched their father depart, snickering in their brute, insolent way when he was safely gone.

And the father often walked in the yard in the moonlit hours, a bottle in his hands; sometimes he toppled into the dust, moaning, and sometimes he slouched upon a stump, and some hours he babbled to himself, or sobbed wordlessly, or moaned, or said some woman's name. How you crept to go to him, but always turned back inside.

III. When you were of age you went into the fields, and there you worked the oxen at their plows. You became calloused and low shouldered, taut and muscled, and soon the hired men dwarfed you no more. And in the afternoons, while the farmer lunched at his table, you crouched on an abandoned cider barrel, telling bawdy jokes while the men praised the depravity of your wit. And you played cards and smoked the tobacco they rolled into papers, the flecks dappling your lips, while the brothers carried forth jugs of ale and the daughter brought crusty lard sandwiches on tarnished tin trays. This girl whose name you knew only from what the breeze carried out, who watched you when she thought you attended to your smoke, your cards, and you noted the dusty swan line of her neck; the pink of her lips, their slight part, the front edges of her teeth hinting there.

And when the work ceased for the night you lay in the moldering hay, in the soft glow of the oil lamp, reading the abandoned schoolbooks of the children of the family, the mud-finger-smudged McGuffey Reader, Aesop's Fables, and Davies's *New Elementary Algebra*, drifting your fingers along the language of these, wondering if the girl had once possessed this one, and were these her marks, and had she once traced her fingers here as you now did, and if you inhaled the yellowing dust of these pages would you inhale also the ghost of what was once her: flecks from the dirt of her travels, the stain of her perspiration, the inflection of her breath; while outside the loose drifts of sand and dust gusted against the windows, and long-off crickets hummed, and wolves moaned from the forest interior. Such were those years, beholden to the slightest gestures of the farmer and his family, to what they called their "generosity," born of their love for the Almighty and of the Almighty's love for all His inventions, great and small.

IV. Yes, in those days all the farmers and the friends of the farmers lived in constant and obsequious dread of the Almighty. Many nights the countryside seemed to burn with the light of the farmers' devotion, the bleating of coming sacrifice, the black smoke of burnt offerings. And what farmer's child by the age of seven had not laid an eviscerated goat before the mountain, or tossed a blood-emptied figure onto a fire and wafted the fumes mountainward? And what farmer did not instruct his child in binding the legs, in slitting the throat and collecting the blood? What farmer did not preach to his child the words to utter, while the animal's consciousness passed into the Almighty's mouth? And what child did not wonder, "Why must we do this?" and what farmer did not respond, "The Almighty is ever hungry." And what man would not say that he would give his only begotten son in this manner to the Almighty, for such is the devotion required of man unto a Father he loves?

And women lit candles in the Almighty's name, uttering the language of devotion, and in kind they bade their children speak His name as they kneeled at the foot of their beds. And what child did not dream the Almighty peering into His copper telescope, witnessing in the immortal lens the beating of their secret blackness? What child has not dreamed His eyes, great and gleaming, when He whispers His commandments unto them, while His sepulchral breath gusts through the valley?

And the thousand doomed pilgrims who climbed the Almighty's black mountain, their walking sticks and bison-hide jackets, their packs stuffed with jerky and casks of water. They smiled to those they loved and waved to those they wished to impress. And into the mists they ventured, gone for days it seemed. And such fools always tumbled down, their grim ghouls faces scorched off and blistered open. And their remains were thrown into potter's fields, or they were buried in yards, and soon bushes thrived above them, sometimes bursting into flame and humming what some considered songs and others dire warnings.

And in those days all dressed in their finest attire and went to the house of worship attended by their neighbors. Here all sought to illustrate the greatness of the love and fear they held within their breasts. So too on Sundays the farmer and his family boarded their wagon at an hour when even the chickens paced and pecked with respect for the calm. You and the other hands followed in a donkey cart, these men fresh shaved at the farmer's instruction, unearthly pale and smooth compared with their otherwise sun-ravaged apparitions. And you men wore your best suits, your only suits, handed down from the farmer, dusty with flecks of hay and other common detritus. And you wore bowler hats or no hats. How stifling was this costume, as if trussed up in a coffin. So your caravan clopped toward the black mountain, and soon other carts and carriages filled with the blazed red faces of men; and the pale, coddled faces of boys in suits and hats; and the pale, sturdy figures of women and girls in dresses and bonnets. Elsewhere along the road and across the fields rode men on horseback. And here other families arrived in their burdened wagons. And here horses snorted and oxen milled in wary silence. And here sacrifices bleated, lambs and goats, and then their guts' slick purple coil, and the bloodstained grasses, and the smoke and crackling. Tents were erected in the center of the field, often red and sometimes blue, sturdy and unwavering no matter the morning winds. And a hundred bodies streamed into the tent while others loitered the edges and children chased each other along the field, jacket tails flapping. So all gathered within: farmers and their families on folding chairs, while servants and hired hands massed along the edges. And the preacher at the fore was perhaps the man from last week, or perhaps that man was caught within some wife or daughter and forced to move along to another county. And while the preacher sermonized he gestured to the black mountain, saying, "Upon yonder hill the Almighty lives and sits and watches us all." And while all others gazed mountainward you watched the girl seated with her family, her blue ribbon and light blond hair; the black blemish upon her neck's long line, marvelously impure; her lips' movement when she turned enough for you to witness them.

V. How many evenings then you watched the daughter in the muted light of her bedroom window, in her dressing gown, and how your fingers played against your shirtsleeve, or the barn door, as if caressing her hair. How those brothers sat smoking on the front porch, the red pulse of their pipes, watching you as you watched her. The note they nailed to the barn wall that read "We will spill your guts to the dust," and below they scrawled what seemed the depiction of one boy murdered by two. So it was you gazed no more upon this girl; no matter, for now you carried her apparition within you always, and the long nights, nestled within your hay, ever drawing her, smearing the lines and refiguring them anew.

This was how you passed the hours when the Almighty first whispered your name. And into the night you were compelled, into the forests beyond the farmer's fields, as if led by a hand unseen, and into the depth of blackness of the forest interior, where around you silent animals observed. Now the Almighty's creature appeared and here the holy beast's full horror: veined wings, and obsidian horns, and hooves of soot, and fur-tufted legs, and its eyes crimson and shining, as if lit by the eternal furnace of His soul. Pine needles sparked and flared, and leaves smoked and blackened. And you could not scream for your throat was constricted. And you could not run for you were frozen in the awesome light. Finally the creature spoke in the sound of choirs burning and trumpets melting, and by this wrathful din it was said you would bring the Almighty's testament to the people. And in the later days of your life and all the days of your death you would be called a man of greatness and a bringer of light. And the creature commanded you to live a life of goodness and purity until it returned with the tablets of the final testament.

Soon you stood before her window, flushed with greatness and clasping a pebble readied to throw. And when her shadow loomed you were to shout her name, but now the only sounds that followed were the crickets and the slowing throb of your heart, and the pebble you now let fall.

VI. And no matter your dreams or intentions you never spoke to this girl, and you never would, for soon a young man from town arrived on horseback—his velvet jacket and bowler hat, his silk ribbon waving, and his substantial whiskers flickering against the rush of breeze. You peered from the barn entrance, and when he called you to hitch his stallion, back into the darkness you slid. That night he dined with the family, and from below the window you listened to silverware clattering on porcelain, the mother's laughter and the father's gruff approval. And from the barn you watched the young man smoke cigars with the farmer, and later when the young man stood outdoors with the daughter, her hand upon the rail and his own soft hand engulfing hers. How you muffled your sobs with the fleshy parts of your hand, and for days afterward you refused your broth, bound yourself in blankets, shivered and wept.

And of your apparent illness the brothers asked their father, "If he dies then may we burn him ourselves?"

VII. Finally you went to the farmer, saying, "I intend to leave all this and seek the wider world," and the farmer said, "Is that right?" He stroked his stubble. He spat into the dust. He said, "After all we have done for you, an orphan in the fields, feeble before the circling birds and wild dogs?" and he sputtered, "How hollow your belly without the food with which we have fattened you!" and he raged, "After we have done for you all any man with a fear of the Almighty could possibly do unto another?" and his eyes said if he held a shovel he would shatter your skull, and if he held a knife he would gouge your belly, and if he held a pitchfork he would impale you into the farmyard. And he said, "Think of your life had we not found you swaddled but with the dust," although other times he said they had found you in the grasses, or in the cornstalks, or surrounded by wild dogs, or in the hunched and swaggering shadows of vultures, or in a basket along the river, or crawling in a ditch, while the final description never wavered: "slick with your own father's blood."

And when you responded without obeisance he again spat, "You are not too old for the switch," and he seethed, "Nor am I too old to deliver it unto you." And you did not test the measure of his words. And you did not spill his blood before the girl, watching from her bedroom window.

VIII. So that night while the farmer and his family slept, you stood beneath the full gauze of the midnight sky, and watched the darkened glass of her window, and you dreamed the figure asleep within. Soon you crept onto the road, your bundle of schoolbooks slung over your shoulder. And now you were alone in the moonlit dirt, with your pulsing heart, your choking breath.

Now the roadside dark was speckled with incandescent eyes and there shone a wilderness of teeth. And with a hand trembling you brandished a knife, and with chattering teeth you spoke the Almighty's name.

And you awaited the long-off bloom of dust foretelling the farmer and his sons, their muskets and snorting horses, and in their eyes, the depth of blackness, the coming of oblivion.

When no dust bloomed you constructed a fire from dead leaves and branches and curled upon the road with your bundle as a pillow. Now you dreamed the Almighty on His mountain and there He seemed a man as any other, in beard and robe, but His eyes flashed fire, and in a voice of thunder He commanded, "Go forth."

Now in this dream you went down from His mountain to the forest of suicides: the white rows of birches, bark flaking like molting flesh, and dead men, hoary with flies, dangling from ropes. Finally you emerged on the edge of a pond. Here deer and rabbit tracks were stamped in the mud while the sun fractured white and violet upon the water. You filled your hands with this bounty while overhead carrion birds circled.

Across the way sat two young men, hunched on a log, their fishing poles bent and tremulous. And the water fractured before them and one called out to the other and they both laughed. So you knew this laughter well. And nowhere present seemed the farmer but in smoke coiling from beyond the forest.

And in this dream the Almighty whispered the brothers' names, although they seemed articulated in an ancient language, and your dream-mind called this language "Hebrew." Now you traveled back through the forest, emerging finally into a clearing where a fire burned and the farmer lay, hands clasped beneath his head. Some distance beyond loomed a smote black house with black pillars, warped and vibrating in the smoking air.

And you dreamed that you took a rock of sharpness and heft from the soil, clung to with moss and dirt, and smelling of the long submergence. And when you heard the faintest snore from the farmer you crept to him.

And from the soil you took this rock and into the skull of the farmer thus you submerged this rock. Thus planted no more would this man moan or speak or dream but bleed, yes, and coagulate, yes, and feed the soil thereafter, yes.

And when you finished you opened your eyes to the blur of the sun. You lay in the road, your heart throbbing and your fire gone to ash. And flies buzzed upon your flesh for you were also red and sticky with the discharge of your atrocity.

IX. You next woke in town, slouched against a shop door, while the shopkeeper glared over you. He said, "Sleep it off elsewhere." And when you asked for work he said, "I have no use for addicts or derelicts." And you stuttered, "I am alone in this world, sir," and you choked back sobs and now said your mother and father were dead.

And this man regarded your blood-spattered clothing, the mess thick in your hair, saying, "Was it natives?" and you said, "Sir?" and he said, "Did natives do this?" And he gestured to a native walking the street: "Did one of those red devils butcher your family?" You looked at the native man unhitching a horse, and you looked at this shopkeeper, and you said, "Yes." And this shopkeeper swore, and he paced, and he swore again, and from his pocket he gathered a flask, and he said, "Well, here," and he bade you drink, and what you had thought would be whisky was only water. How you drank it anyway. And when the shopkeeper asked your name you invented the name the world knows you as. Now when this shopkeeper asked if you could stand, you said, "Of course," but you fell in a lump, so the shopkeeper hoisted you, and now when he asked, "Can you walk?" you answered, "Of course," and now you hobbled against him with legs of rubber.

Now the shopkeeper brought you to his house, and there he instructed you to bathe. You simply looked at him. So he showed you how to operate the faucet, turning one knob and saying, "This is for cool water," and then turning the opposite knob and saying, "This is for hot water." And you said you had never known there was more than one kind. And now he handed you a bar of soap and you gazed at it as if it were of alien manufacture, and he said, "You bring this over your figure, as thus," and he pantomimed the bathing process. When you submerged yourself the clear water filled black with blood and dirt, and your body seemed to bob, weightless, and you let out a soft moan and your lids closed, the water rising and falling against your chin. And when you finished the shopkeeper brought a pair of shears, for by this time your hair fell to your shoulders, greatly tangled with hay and lice and fleas and all the sordid insects of the barn. The shopkeeper dispatched your locks to the floor with much pulling and grunting, and with this concluded he brought you to a bedroom. The walls of this room were white and bare save those bookshelves, dusty and empty, and these you ran your finger across. After some silence the shopkeeper said, "This was my son's room," and of this matter he said no more, and so you indicated the bed, primly made and unused in some while, saying, "I've never seen one of those before..." and after a pause you finished, "... except in books."

X. At his shop, he made you watch his every endeavor, and soon he bade you mimic him and you did. And there were customers who exclaimed, "Why, this isn't Harvey!" meaning the old hired lad, gone west as so many before. And there were those who said, "He seems the spitting image of John," and you would learn they meant the shopkeeper's son. To these customers he said nothing, although later you saw he chewed his lip until it bled.

And when the shopkeeper busied himself with those who mobbed him for the gossip of the day or the politics of the moment or even the speculations on the potato market, you lost yourself in your investigations, wandering the store and the back room, the mice dead in their traps, their bloody teeth; the barrels and burlap sacks slouched against the walls stuffed with dried beans and corn and rice, how you sifted your hands into these; the casks of root beer; the boxes of potatoes and carrots and snap peas and string beans and beets and rutabaga yet black with soil; and everywhere the pungency of leather from boots and shoes and belts there displayed, and walls were hung with wrought-iron pots and pans, and the shelves lined with lamps and stacked with dyed cloth, canned pears and peaches and beans and beets and tomatoes, and these you shook against your ear, as if the fluid within could speak its mystery.

Now the life you made within this store, the bow tie you wore and adjusted and readjusted, the pencil you slid behind your ear, the tip you wet when jotting calculations. How you soon knew the names of all who came before you and they called you "sir," and you told them jokes about the weather or the politics of the day. And a great many customers wandered through his shop, farmers and their sons and their hired men, and always afterward the stinking track from their boots. And always you thought of the farmer and his sons, although with each day such thoughts dulled. Natives too passed through the doors, and some dressed as a white man dresses, and some dressed yet in their buckskins, and some wore feathers, and others simply wore their long hair braided, and the shopkeeper observed these men as a farmer observes a cloud of locusts. And many women wandered through the doors, or those who wished for you to meet with women wandered through, who asked of you, "When will you be stopping over?" for their daughter Marie or Sara or Claire would certainly love to meet a young man of such "fine determination," and you blushed and averted your eyes. And soon it was that even the elders who passed before you brought forth their daughters, unwed and aging, often smiling, sometimes forced near sneers, and other times only too eager, lascivious. And there were those women dressed entirely in black, and their eyes seemed to linger the longest and their fingers seemed to brush against yours the most, while you blushed and mumbled some witticism about the potato market.

And there were those men in rumpled suits and well-worn shoes and dusty hats who walked through the doors with "items" they wished to sell to the shop, antiaging creams and pills and potions and liquors in bottles labeled "Elixir" and "Miracle Agent" and "Eternal Youth." And these men sometimes gave their full pitch wherein they claimed the aged would regain the color of their hair and their teeth would re-form from their bloody, gaping gums, and those who walked stooped as cripples would straighten their backs, and those who could not walk would learn to walk anew, and those with milky eyes would know their vision cleared, and those with no memories would again recall all they had known and loved. And sometimes these pitches came in the form of "yarns" they "spun" about "real folks" who had prospered by these miracle cures, derived from native recipes forgotten by the modern world. "We think because we have the steam engine that we have all the answers, but it isn't so. The common people of the land, the native folk of these areas, they were in touch with answers we don't even know the questions to." And other times there came a song, perhaps a banjo tune or two, and sometimes a woman sang and a child danced, or an outfitted monkey clanged symbols, or some dog stood upright, hopping in circles as if deranged. And some days the shopkeeper allowed this business, and other times when he heard the carriages approach by the hee-hawing of their mules or the tinkling of their cans, he fended them off with a broom or he brandished his rifle, and sometimes they came forth no matter his objections, saying, "When you find out what I have in these here cases you'll thank me for stopping," and sometimes it took one shot into the air, and sometimes it took two, and very often it took three. And of these men the shopkeeper often said, "Never turn your back, for such men would gladly see the both of us dead and this shop entire cluttered with their wares." And when you smiled the shopkeeper said, "You listen to me," and when you said, "Who would want a shop filled with trinkets and absurdities?" he responded, "Most of the men and women of this country."

For in those days the nation was known as a land of coming splendor, a land of young men on the make, and into those mysterious western places many a second son and orphan went, seeking his fortune. And what farm boy or wandering orphan did not dream himself dressed as a millionaire, in top hat and tapping out his way with a diamond-headed cane? And no matter the western beat of heathen drums, for what honest white man did not long to eradicate the natives in favor of shops and schools, factories and churches?

And when he found you reading dusty volumes from his shelves, yawning for their dullness as these contained mostly letters and decrees composed by politicians and sermons composed by preachers, this shopkeeper insisted you set them aside. "There are those who say we have no literature in this country," he said. "They are wrong, for within these pages we find the great truths of all our nation, we find the language of our coming greatness." And now he brought you certain magazines and newspapers, and within those pages you found ads for encyclopedias and dictionaries and travel magazines; and hand-wrought jewelry; and gold watches certain to keep time no matter the wear and damage of the piece; and life insurance; and galvanized iron roofing; and internal flushings to eliminate "all waste and disease from the bodily system";

and fertile chicken eggs; and counterirritants for rheumatism, gout, stiff joints; and matchless cigar lighters; and books purporting to explain the "science of Life and Self-Preservation"; and notebook holders and ink stands; and bust enhancers and waist shapers; and imported tea sets decorated with cocks and hens; and typewriters guaranteed to save all from "your pen-scribbled puzzles"; and cures for stammering; and steampowered threshers and mowing machines; and soothing syrups for wind colic and the unstable bowels of teething infants; and foolproof serums for the devastated kidneys and liver of addicts and drinkers; and elixirs guaranteed to perpetuate the loveliness of new carpets; and one hundred doses of "vital sparks" syrup to stimulate a man to "red-blooded vitality" and return the aging "gentleman" to "glorious youth"; and oil lamps and oil lubricants and oil lozenges and oil jellies; and country homes in unknown and unsettled lands; and rye whisky; and electricity machines guaranteed to return eyesight and hearing and cure headaches, neuralgia, bronchitis, weak lungs, and "waning virility" (thus a man was shown wired to this machine while lightning flashed and in the next illustration he was shown well muscled and juggling bowling pins); and cures for weak ankles; and lawyers for "all domestic relations"; and hand-tailored "vogue hats"; and companies promising to deliver "lettuce salad daily"; and soaps for the complexion and soaps for the aging; and apple jellies; and Turkish cigarettes (and here were belly dancers with rounded hips and tantalizing bellies); and books guaranteed to illuminate the mysteries of the meat industry; and dolls for the children; and there were scores upon scores of ads for still more catalogs and brochures and pamphlets. So you cut these ads from the papers and slathered them with glue and spread them along the walls of the bedroom, and when there was no more room you plastered them upon the ceiling, and when there was no more room upon the ceiling you glued them into notebooks. How often you gazed at the walls and the ceiling, transfixed by these weird marvels and the illustrations that bent them into some kind of reality, the language that made their accomplishments almost tangible.

And so it was this shopkeeper who said, "There will come a time when the only story a man may read in this nation will stand plastered on the walls of his favorite tavern or slathered onto the sides of the carriages in the streets, and it will be written in such a language as all men may understand and not simply those few." And it was this shopkeeper who said, "Soon all men of this land may know and comprehend the plain and simple language of another."

XI. And often there were those who peddled wares not for the flesh but for the eternal soul as prescribed by the Almighty, for in the progress of this new nation all faiths seemed possible, and all manifestations of the Creator seemed true. Now there were those who gathered in the forests and bathed in the rivers, and so many playing children were unwittingly greeted by the pale, liberated flesh of the godly— oh, to be a lad before that wilting and corpulence, to feel the breath quicken as a sagged woman coos from the brush, or a flaccid man pleads for a roll in the needles and leaves. Oh, to believe with deepest faith that in another's flesh one finds the Almighty's light! And there were those who would not murder or eat the flesh of animals, gnawing upon only what they found growing from the land. And there were those who uncovered the flesh of men buried, and these were seen wandering with burlap sacks and crowbars and sniffing at the soil. And there were those who lived twelve or more within the same house and worked no jobs, choosing rather to till the soil and raise livestock, to feast upon the bounty of their labor. And here the men slept in rooms across from the women, but no sex frolicked with the other, for to fornicate was considered the foulest sin. And now pregnant women were excommunicated and sent to live amongst the sinners of the land while the implanter of the seed was but reprimanded, for "a man's lusts are the deepest of all nature's transgressions" and it was well known that "the female encourages and lures the male." And some called for an end to priests, for one man should not stand as gatekeeper to another man's salvation.

And some called the natives the "wandering tribes" of the original peoples. And some found in caves and under rotten stumps tablets writ with the language of the Almighty.

And there were men who drifted from church to church, from movement to movement, and from tavern to tavern, finding no solace for that which burned their soul, the torment and doubt. And when all faiths and tonics were exhausted they were found slouched against boulders, their heads blown out, pistols fallen to their chests, or they dangled from the trees, their necks rope-burned red, and black tongues distended. So many gave up their flesh beneath His black mountain that medical students traded the graveyard for this forest when seeking fresh corpses. And schoolchildren dared their chums to gaze upon the ghoulish decompositions, the souls struggling free, diaphanous, and wandering mountainward.

And many who did not put the pistol to their mouth found relief in lashing themselves, so parading the forests and streets, moaning and spilling black blood, while stray dogs and cats trotted at a careful distance, lapping the red tide. Or they found relief in those who preached the end of time, the final date named, and congregations made to renounce all possessions (although many of these preachers and followers invariably did kill themselves rather than admit the folly of false hopes). Indeed, how many false revelators were dragged through the streets, the cobbles strewn with bloody scraps of preacher's garb? And others fled in the dead night for new towns, where their shame was not yet known, and there they named some new date of final doom, now again entirely certain to come.

Yes, you knew these preachers, in all their names and guises. They attempted to infiltrate the shopkeeper's home and the shopkeeper's shop, to explain the days and why they were made, and when the world would fall to a final night. You heard them speak the words of the Almighty, and you saw them in the forests of the land, praying unto the trees, gathering up the moss and the sticks and calling them the voice of God, or you saw them at the golden altars of their churches, decrying all other churches and preachers as the utterers of ignorance and sin. And when in the presence of no one else you told these preachers, "His creature has visited me in the night and bathed me in its terrible light," and they replied, "Sure it did," or "You all right, son?" or "You mocking me?"

And middle-class preachers preached in their own parlors, coffee and tea and cakes provided afterward by their wives, and poor preachers preached in town squares and on stoops, in tin sheds and in wooden shacks, and here they shouted their twisted impressions of holy books known to all. By this time a thousand preachers of a thousand configurations wandered the streets, and some promised ruination and the rise of devils and a "great roasting," while others pledged cities in the clouds, and others promised choirs of creatures, and others said there was no end or beginning, for all lived within the same constant breath of life. And no matter the nature of their inclinations or the origin of their holy insights, all insisted upon tithes and donations of possessions. Indeed many preachers wept openly at collection plates heaped with silver coins and watches and pearl necklaces and gold teeth, and later they slept upon these riches, or filled tubs with coins and jewels and bathed in them. And many were run out of town with shotguns and pitchforks, and others were feathered and run out of town straddling rails, the fumes of scorched skin and tar, white eyes beneath the morass. And many built enormous houses with gold fountains on the front lawn, naked children spitting water, and these preachers too were run out of town, or strung up, or filled with boiling silver or lead, for none could suffer a charlatan in those days.

And you walked in their midst, listening to all. And it is said you learned much of the world from these men.

XII. And the shopkeeper simply said, "There is no world beyond the one you see here," gesturing to the shop, the goods, and the advertisements adorning the walls. And when you asked why he owned their books he replied, "If you understand the language these men speak, you will also know how to sell them goods." And when you indicated the black mountain this shopkeeper said, "Son, there's no man living on that mountain. And if there is, I promise you His will does not make this world turn."

And this shopkeeper insisted you dress in the fashion he desired, and he insisted you keep your face clean of whiskers and your hair short and tidy, and he sometimes asked of you, "May I call you 'son'?" You never could say otherwise to this man. And he told you the books to read and the philosophies to espouse and the dreams to place burden upon, for this shopkeeper openly explained his sole ambition in these final days was to see you take over the shop "when I'm safely moldering in the ground."

And this shopkeeper brought you the daily paper illustrated with the great finding of the day—some enormous and terrible lizard a hundred million years dead and buried, transfigured into bone and stone and now dug up. "This creature and its entire species was born and died before your black mountain was dreamed." And you spat upon the man and you tore the paper in two and cast the fragments to the wind. "You see what I think of your stories," you said.

XIII. And now when you and the shopkeeper closed shop for the night you said, "I have small business to attend to," rather than return home with him. And the shopkeeper winced, saying, "Well, do what you must, but hurry back then." And these hours you spent along the alleyways laughing and drinking whisky from flasks and puffing cigars with peddlers, their slouch hats and yellow eyes and seldom teeth. And these men explained their potions were concocted with no magic but the bounty of alcohols and common herbs and cocaine and sugar—yes, to you and your wide eyes they explained the secrets of their methods without hesitation—and you listened in silence, your only motion of interest a slight nod. And they explained the mystic wisdom of the natives, the fear of the heavens, the looming horror of all disease, and how "all folks believe deep down there's a better land, and that long ago we lived in such a better land," and "some believe this is a place of the earth" and "some say it is a land divine," and you said, "—on top of the black mountain," and they said, "Some would have it so. More folks in this particular valley than anywhere else we've seen."

And some days you crept to the perimeter of revival tents. Now while others sang and swayed within those red-and-white-striped skins, you lingered at grog stalls, drinking deep of what seemed meant to clean paint from the walls. How your throat blazed and your eyes livened. You tossed your last coins onto the table and shook your empty cup at the vendors, while ever in the background droned the preacher's furious, intoxicating chants. Here you watched always for the farmer, his wife, his sons, and here you waited for the daughter, the line of her neck, her high laugh. And when you believed you saw the brothers or the farmer, you followed them, plucking a branch from the ground in your stride. So in these times thoughts of murder alone trespassed your mind.

And when you did not find these brothers you returned to the stalls, and now lost in the fumes of drink you wept, describing the lines of her neck and confessing your secret hopes and transgressions.

How beautiful the burn of the grog, the grip of the fumes, and you swayed as you drank, while preachers and peddlers lectured on their travels, on their dreams. How often these men spoke words like "respectable" and "society," for in those days even a man with three teeth in all his mouth dreamed of seating himself amongst the tables of the wealthiest and most prestigious society. And you cheered and toasted them and you cried out, "How right you are! How right you are!"

And after these revivals you often found yourself moaning and half asleep in a ditch, sticky with dew and the saliva of malefactors unknown. And there were nights you found yourself in a nameless woman's arms, her black teeth and breath of rot. And there were nights you woke slouched against a tree with your pockets rifled through, and other nights you staggered home stinking of grog and piss and the Word of God. And some nights the shopkeeper who called himself "Father" waited for you, feigning to read by candlelight. And some nights he only ground his teeth, his face pulsing red, and would not speak. And some nights he was unable to meet your gaze and you were unable to meet his. And some nights the kitchen floor was strewn with broken plates and the shopkeeper was passed out in some corner of the house. And some nights you sneered at him, snoring, a bottle of bourbon clutched to his chest. And some nights you covered his prone boozy body with a blanket. And some nights you fell into his arms weeping.

No matter. Each night you continued on with these men. Nothing more luxuriant than a preacher in new silk robes leading a young woman to his tent for "prayers." Little seemed more fabulous than the murky vials of peddlers, mundane elements churned into elixirs and charms, cure-alls and tonics, common ingredients made to carry the breath of God.

XIV. One morning the shopkeeper awaited you at his front stoop. His face was slouched and gray, and when he attempted to speak now you told him of a world newly born before you. You told him how the very night before, while a preacher ranted and bonfires blazed, you staggered into the forest. Here you traversed a moonlit stream, slipped on moss-slick rocks, and stumbled over rotten limbs and decaying birch trunks, and soon you lay moaning in the muck. So you remained until a soft light glowed overhead. And the ground pulled open and the soil swirled into a pool of fire, and there gnashed and writhed a million damned. And from the fires rose the creature you had known in your boyhood, its sharp glinting hooves and dense obsidian tongue. And when the creature cried for you to repent you fell to your knees—"Is that so?" said the shopkeeper—and the creature led you to a dank and putrid cave where the bleached skulls of many animals lay, and within this darkness were the golden tablets of the Almighty's final word. "It is time you knew the fullness of your destiny," the creature brayed. And when the shopkeeper wondered, "And where are these tablets?" you shrugged. "The dread beast chastised me as a backslider and said I could not see them for many years. I must make for myself first a holy life." So the shopkeeper cried, "How you break my heart!" and he wept, "You would rather see me dead than call me 'Father.'"

And you mentioned no more to the shopkeeper of such a visitation.

XV. Now there were nights you did not return to his house. On the first such night the shopkeeper waited in the glow of his lantern, his voice like a sob when you entered at dawn, asking if you were hungry or if you needed new clothes, for you now wore little more than rags. You merely sneered and called him a fool. From then on he awaited your arrival from his bedroom window and listened to your comings and goings and all your movements in between through the floor. In time then he would know you by your tracks and handprints alone, for you trailed dirt wherever you went, and your hands were always gray with dried mud.

XVI. Each night now you ventured forth with four men—orphans such as you, come from farms to seek the wider world—and you knew them well by their cigars and pipes, slouch hats and beards. And since many men sought their fortunes through the finding of treasure, you told them you had acquired what you called a seer's stone, saying, "It produces for me a great diminishment of space," and "I have peered through all manners of material into the secrets housed therein."

And you each spun stories of the fortunes you would make, the possessions you would obtain. And you said, "Finally, I will be quit of this damned shopkeeper."

And one man worked as a farmhand, and he desired to be free of the plow and spend his hours "within the whores." And two others pitched wares, "exotic" creams and lotions, boiled roots mashed into "antiaging elixirs." And another man lived immersed in "ancient" maps, scouring the valleys, the riverbeds, the mountains, digging holes as deep as a man is tall, sifting the silt and sand. Ever thwarted in his endeavors, now you placed your hand upon his bosom, saying, "The end of your failures is nigh, my friend."

When you had coins you slept in boardinghouses, and when you did not you crept into barns, and there rats and fleas, and there the indomitable quiet of cattle. Now in the hours before dream you rhapsodized of the fortunes to come, and you joked of the wealthy men you had known, how their riches bought them "water flowing right into their houses" and how "this water was as hot or as cold as you could want," and "they sleep on beds as light and airy as the clouds themselves," and "when they desire a steak someone fixes them a steak" and "when they desire fancy potatoes someone fixes them fancy potatoes." And you spoke of the cigars the wealthy smoked, the brandy they drank, the magnificent burn, "how smooth and luxurious his liquor is compared with our own." And you joked about the wealthy man's laziness, his cruelty and indifference, and you clapped your friends warmly upon the backs, saying, "That will be each of us, soon enough, if you have faith in my stone." And to a man they murmured they would follow you unto the ends of the earth.

XVII. Now you scoured the land, investigating every farm and field, hillside and cave, and when the skies blackened you fled to dark forests, where bloated suicides swung like enormous cocoons and wolves in their caverns dreamed of murder. In the winds and rain, shivering and starving, you spoke of chests of gold hidden in caves, or the barren husks of oaks. And you said sacks of gold dwelled at the bottom of wells. And you said, "The great explorers of old found such riches on these shores as never before conceived." And when your comrades wondered why those settlers had never retrieved their buried fortunes, you explained a great many forces, seen and unseen, had murdered them.

Ever the days, then, seated before fires, eyes blurry and lustful, unfurling ancient maps and sketching new maps, weighing and measuring and calculating the illustrated X where treasure surely lay. When in dank caverns and gloomy forests you found the place marked X you commanded, "Dig," and the very soil exhaled from the split earth. Into the ground these men went, lost within the mania of their toil. And they hefted out muck and rocks, bones and skulls, with sacks fashioned from their clothing. And when no man recovered treasure they insisted some force must have removed the riches, for they had envisioned gold glittering out of reach. And at each of these pronouncements, at every inexplicable failure, you cried, "See that trail of soot? Brothers, the Evil One has again played us for fools."

You were soon infamous, covered always in soil and stink and paying your bills in promises, but all men dream of a greater world and many fellows with moth-chewed maps and family legends commissioned your talents. And many raved of your skill, claimed you found marvels and riches and heaps of jewels and fascinating artifacts, while others insisted any man who hired you was being duped. Flush for the first in your lives, who in your small and fragile clan did not spread the coins of his bounty before his bed? And when you said, "There is much more where that comes from," they looked upon you with great affection, called you "Boss," and named your peeping stone the "Sacred Rock."

And in taverns, the Hog's Head and the Bristled Cow, you made your name as a great player of cards. Here your eye was often blackened as a cheat's, yet you were beloved by almost all, and here they called you "a most vivid personality" and "the fellow most likely to tell the bawdiest jokes and sing the loudest songs." And so you sang, and so you drank, and how often did they find you retching in the street, and how many strange women did you cling to in these bottomless and ill-remembered nights? And did you know regret in your soul, or did you lust only for the night, to return to those women, hoary and ragged and groaning, and some merely seeming to be women?

And when the money was gone, you camped in fields and forests, slumped in alleyways and slumbered on benches, and you fell into the arms of widows and women of poor repute. And to the whores you left what coins you had, and when you had no coins you paid in "promissory notes." Hollow payments that left you spitting blood, cast into the street by pimps who knew only the language of murder.

And you stayed in boardinghouses and in the homes of Samaritans, kindly men and women who feared the blackness of His mountain and the depth of His horrid soul. Here you men shared a room: you tucked into the bed while another man nested in a velvet armchair, his ragged hat slouched over his brow, and the other two curled with each other on the floor, arms haphazardly tossed over bodies, stained undershirts or no shirts, faces nuzzled into shoulders, whiskered cheek mashed to whiskered cheek. In those nights the smell of one man mingled easily with the smell of another, and what man did not dream lonesome and needy thoughts of the man pressed into him, breathing faintly into his ear?

And if one cracked the window to let free their musk, then surely you heard the sounds of the wolves from the forests and none could sleep for the tightening of his blood gone cold—

And did you gaze upon these fellows in the light of the moon, knowing you could never sleep with them while you possessed the stone? And did you watch them believing they prayed for your demise, a busted bottle lodged in your throat, a pool of black blood on some beer-sloppy floor, or splayed across sweat- and semen-slick sheets, drained of blood by a pimp's knife while the whore emptied your wallet?

Did they plot to slit your neck, to remove this glass marvel from your open and cooling hands? And what fortunes would they acquire while you lay moldering in a potter's field?

Yes, how could you sleep with these men, or seek treasure in their creeping presence, when coming doom pressed constant upon your skull? Your life now in wait for the shovel blow, your skull burst and bleeding and your flesh a cooling husk. Your dead eyes open while your friends fleece the stone. And perhaps they would bury you in a shallow grave, or perhaps they would leave your corpse for wolves and birds. No, you could not; surely you could not so much as drink the coffee they brewed for even this seemed laced with lye.

And did such thoughts come from your mind or from the voice of the creature you said visited your bed? Whose mouth twisted from the ceiling and dripped a substance unknown unto your very soul, and then a blistering and a crackling, and when you screamed there came no sound but a rattling from the bottom of your throat.

And what of the morning you said you would seek treasure no more? When you bequeathed those men your stone and sent them down the dusted road. How fat their eyes, how their hands shook, even after you said, "It will give no power unto you." They took it anyhow. Then the distant year when you saw them strung from posts, your destiny shown in their limp, swinging figures had you not cast off their sordid lot.

XVIII. You remained in the room, although soon you could no longer afford the luxury. And you prepared letters to the shopkeeper, some requesting funds, some begging forgiveness, some attesting to your "love" for the man you now called "Father." And these you never sent. These you lit with your candle, and the language of your endearment flickered and curled into oblivion.

Soon you returned to taking commissions, and it was said even without your artifact you retained your prior skill. Now you pointed mere branches toward the fields, called them "divining rods" and followed their indication at a trot, as if led by some invisible hound. And when you found water or silver or boulders apparently illustrated in chalk with images of chests of gold or wealthy ancient peoples, there were those who praised your insight. And there were those who paid you double to replicate your success. And there were those who said you planted some findings, and fluke luck provided the rest. And some days you were made to return your fees, and some days you were bloodied into the dust, and some days you were brought before the courts and made to defend your manner of business. Ever you persisted in your industry, no matter the weariness that came, for no force could ever make you labor like other men.

XIX. And many days you walked the cobbled streets and alleyways. And you knew much of the flies and the muck, and you knew much of the manure and the silent chewing of horses, the low tails of dogs dining at the refuse-lined gutters. And the ladies who lifted their skirts for the piling of filth and the university-educated priests who were loath to tread where their congregation had trod, the finery of their gowns, the whiteness of their collars, and you saw these men, prim and gallant in their carriages, laughing and carrying on with the comeliest ladies of the congregation.

And you saw much of the sooty-faced urchins, hunkered on wharves and scrounging in alleyways, smoking butts and snapping open the discarded bones of some rich man's lunch, sucking the marrow, or gazing sullen eyed from orphanage windows, longing to fashion a rope from bedclothes. And what child, vagrant and wild, did not pelt you with rotten fruit as you drifted along, or flash his penknife, or lift your wallet? And when you did not box his ears, when you took him aside and lectured on the Almighty's benevolence, did he not spit on you and scamper to meet his brothers?

And you saw civilized natives dressed in the white man's clothes, praying to the Almighty in the white man's manner, while wild natives prayed to their own gods, shaped as foxes and eagles and deer. For a fee these natives led you to ancient depictions of horned beasts and bears and wolves, images drawn into the rocks of the forests. Images originating from the days when men and animals strode together, intermarrying and breeding, and in this time men grew wings and walked with hooves, horns glinting from their skulls. And the natives said in the original design men and animals knew no separation. In those days all flesh had been as one.

And you walked the corridors of the Museum of Natural History, where all manner of beasts were posed in perpetual snarl and glassy stare. How fathers and sons gaped at brown bears and lions and elephants, stiff and sawdust stuffed, impervious to decay and the motions of time. And you stood before the erected bones of a long-dead monster. The creature towered over all, and through the vacant socket one saw only darkness in place of what had been. Men and women came and went, chattering while you remained motionless, your face as if burning. The ribs bones and the absence of where once beat the heart. How the teeth must have brutalized all. Entire species butchered and consumed here. And no man had ever coupled with this horror. No words ever left those long-eradicated lips but pure sounds, roaring and gnashing and oblivion. And when a whiskered man in a bowler hat said to the woman beside him, "This thing died a billion years ago," you sneered, "It's a damned lie." And at this couple, wide eyed and moving away, you wagged your fist: "You should be more careful how you blaspheme His name."

XX. And what of this family you lodged with, the mother and father you heard arguing through the floor. The father, a butcher, who stank of bones and meat, of blood stickiness and flies, who wanted you cast into the street, and the mother who wanted only your money, and their daughter, who danced in the yard amidst the swirling leaves and dust, her skirts twirling as she twirled. How you feared she would snap in her contortions, so slender and pale was she in those days. This girl who seemed somehow Spanish, with her black hair and her dark brown eyes, who gazed upon her shoes when you stood before her, and when you said, "That is a lovely bow in your hair," or "How this dress compliments your complexion," she murmured her thanks. Somehow you knew better than to touch her chin and bring her gaze unto your own.

The woman who cleaned the manure and dust from your shoes, who brought them shined each morning, and each evening set a plate of stewed beef and potatoes and cabbage and carrots before your door. This food you ate while sitting on the edge of your bed, gazing into a streaked and tarnished mirror, and the man who returned your gaze no longer resembled any man you had known. Nights you ventured out, along the piss-stinking mud of alleyways and the sawdust floors of taverns, no longer drinking or gambling, for now you merely gazed upon men in the thrall of excess and sin. And when the wrinkled whores, their liver spots smeared with powders and paint, batted their fat black lashes and slurred, "What would you like, honey?" you sat rigid and cold, finally muttering bawdy jokes until they left.

So you continued until the butcher took you aside, whispering, "Your gambling and whores bring a sickness into my home." He took you by the shirt, seething, his eyes trembling with redness, before finally he pushed you away. Not until he departed did you wipe his spittle from your brow.

XXI. And when one night the mother was ill, their daughter brought boiled potatoes, her tied-up hair, those strands fallen along her brow, her cream pallor and averted eyes. You asked, "Is your father aware you brought these?" When she said nothing, you continued: "He finds me undesirable." The girl barely nodded. And you said, "What do you think?" Finally, she spoke: "I suppose I wouldn't know"— and then, slowly, her eyes along the length of your fingers, the bones of your hand—"Mother doesn't think you're so terrible." And now when she looked down you touched her chin, bringing her gaze to your own, the rise and fall of her chest in the dim oil light.

And every morning thereafter you waited for her at the door. Mutely she brought your shoes, shined and spotless, and when you complimented her work, she pulled away again, watching only the shadow spread before you. Each morning she arrived earlier and earlier, and always you woke to her feet creaking the floorboards and always you stood before her in some condition of wakefulness. Soon there came then the morning her fingers brushed against yours, and now she dared to look upon your hand, and now she dared to look upon your neck, and now the sudden moistness as she licked the plump pinkness of her bottom lip.

And soon she brought your meals, lingering as you ate, and often she hummed for you some pretty melody, her sense of tune as if mountain-sent. And when you learned she played the flute, you requested a performance until she pantomimed the action, her closed eyes and furious blush. How you praised first her nimble fingers, and now you took these in hand, and they were cold, moist, and then you whispered of her beautiful flush, your hand now to her skin, and how it burned and burned. And these mornings you told her of your life: the shopkeeper and the grog stalls, the seer's stone and the girl you said gave it to you, "the prettiest girl I ever saw... until you."

And you explained your fate as bestowed by the creature of the Almighty, the terrible restlessness you felt. And you gestured to the room around you, saying, "I have tarried with bad men, I have misspent my days; what of my soul when the beast returns for me?"

She laid her hands upon yours and there they smoldered. "He knows you are a good man, even if you do not," and she looked away before concluding, "As do I..." There her hands remained, until her mother bellowed from below. Soon you were alone, and then you were not, for the butcher swayed in the doorway, his drunk eyes swiveling within his skull. "Care for a smoke?" he said, and you could not meet his gaze. "A drink then?" and when you knew no joke about liquor you murmured, "No, sir." The butcher nodded. "You will walk with me then." Now you followed him to the yard, where the elms stood black and withering and everywhere the fragrance of their decay. The butcher tottered and hiccupped and finally he said, "I don't care what your intentions are toward my daughter—with men like you it amounts to one sort anyhow." And when you did not respond he gestured at a hunched, misshapen elm: "If you look upon my daughter again I will see you buried beneath yonder sycamores." You trembled and your face burned in that fragile silence, and only after he whispered, "Please," could you look at the man in his weakness. His eyes welled and his mouth hung open. And now you smiled.

And the girl's face shone through her bedroom window, pale and smudged with tears, her mother's shape looming in the shadows behind.

XXII. That night she stood in the dust of the long dirt road, bound up in her arms, in the frailty of her gown. How she smiled when she saw you, as if she would dart, or melt, or disappear into the mist. And you held her, whispering, "The creature has decreed we must go forth into the world." How strange her moonlit eyes, when she trembled against you, crying, "Oh, my dearest," in what had been a child's voice, in a voice no longer her own. Now her lips mashed against your cheeks, and your throat, and, finally, your lips. So you took her from her home, your few possessions wrapped in canvas and bound to your back, and in the morning you were married at the courthouse before a white-haired servant of the law, his smudged spectacles and yellow teeth. There you slid a gold band over her finger—"My one remnant of Mother." And afterward, in the dung-and-straw-strewn streets, you held this girl as she sobbed into your chest.

XXIII. You carried your bride across a threshold of long grasses, for your marriage bed awaited in grain fields. And here you constructed a deer-hide tent. So the natives regarded you from the birch bark forest, and when your wife grew fearful of their drums and the smoke coiling from the forest interior, you explained you would build a cabin "where no heathen will dare trespass." You told her of the days to follow: your ceaseless toil, chopping and hauling and constructing, while she would gather nuts and berries in the day and prepare dinner in the evening. And when you wearied of this game you rested your head upon her lap and told her of the Almighty and His creature, and how someday they would raise you above all other men.

XXIV. Now in the darkness of your tent you knew only your wife, her lips and skin, the sound of her voice. And when she said, "You will tire of me," you kissed her brow, and when she said, "Do not tarry with questionable men," you insisted she had silenced the rowdiness within your soul. And in these nights you wanted nothing of God or His works, for you desired only to lie within her. You told her, "My only city shall be the city we build here."

XXV. In the early days you went into town for goods, and there the men whispered of the "infamy" of your union. You returned with an ax and a saw and bundles of rope, and when you confessed your journey to your wife you never spoke of the way both men and women gossiped, the way you bristled to hear the names they gave her. In the morning you left her, and now you spent many hours within the woods, hacking and resting on the handle of your ax, watching the bugs in the dirt and the leaves, listening to the birds, stripping the bark in near-transparent sheets, lacing your fingers behind your head and napping against a sturdy birch, before finally returning in the dim light, raving of the great work you had accomplished and how your house was "within reach."

And when you cooked the meat of a recent kill you left the tent pulled open, and there your wife lay in the glow of the flame. And you followed the smoke drifting by her bare shoulders, the shadowed rise of her buttocks as if dipped in ink. How your breath caught and she turned to watch you work. How her eyes seemed lost for the dark, for the smoke, for the fumes of the rabbit you roasted on dripping spits. And when you left the tent open through the night, the long fingers of the misty dawn chilled your flesh, and now you held each other, tight and shivering, the chattering of her teeth, and now you warmed her goosefleshed figure with your hands and kisses. How she scarcely stirred against a new dawn and then the soft moan when you kissed her neck. How with your tongue you drew houses and roads and schoolhouses on her belly, her breasts, depicted the children you dreamed to create and name, and the shape of all the days you longed to know with her.

And there were evenings when the distant grasses seemed to glint with the eyes of natives.

And there were days you returned to the forest after a lapse, first of a day, and then after several days, and then after a week. And then more weeks, and finally you dragged the logs into the field. There they lay, strewn, while you slept, exhausted and drenched with sweat.

And there were days the logs swelled and rotted and moldered while you held your beloved tight, whispering of the world to come.

And when the weather cooled you wandered the forests for abandoned cabins. You found them with roofs caved in or the rotten walls collapsed, and the doors ajar or no doors at all. And within these weathered constructions you often found bodies, decomposed and mere skeletons, what were once parents holding what were once children, the carpets and walls splattered with brown blood. And in others you found only blood patterned in secret testimonies of horror. And here you found dusty and unopened cans of beans and peaches, and you found the nests of birds, and you found the ancient droppings of bears and wild cats, and from certain corners came low growls and yellow eyes.

XXVI. And on the forest floor you found the remains of a man. Above him a rope yet dangled from the branches while a note, wilted and blurred beyond comprehension, was nailed to the trunk. How you observed the flesh, mostly now eaten away, the pale bone and empty sockets, the tattered coat and trousers, shoes removed and placed neatly to the side and a pocket watch placed within. Your hand trembled to touch the smoothness of what remained, where neither bug nor creature clattered anymore within. How you said, "Did you have no father? Did you never know the name of God? Did no woman ever love you and was no child ever born of your flesh?" And no answer came from the once man, nor did any response follow from the mountain.

XXVII. And some days you made the pretense of stacking and arranging what remained of the logs, although soon you sighed and instead wandered the forest. And while you worked, your wife drew figures in the dirt, smearing them out when you returned. And she said, "We should move into one of those cabins," and after some silence you almost said, "The other cabins are unlivable," and you almost

said, "I believe men and women have been murdered in them," and you nearly said, "I would fear for our safety, even more, because we could not see them coming," but instead you said, "These walls provide the only shelter we need. For the Almighty's creature watches over us." And when your wife fantasized about a house in town, desiring the presence of markets and the society of others, you gestured to the forest, saying, "Here is enough to quench our earthly longings." She averted her eyes: "Of course, your love is the only community I want, my darling," and placing your hand upon her belly, the warm, smooth flesh, she said, "But what if I was with child?" And you lay beside her: "His creature will watch over the child too." And your wife continued: "What would we name him?" And you said, "Him?" And she nodded, so you said the name you claimed as your father's. And she said, "How would he appear?" and you described your own shape and you described the shape of the man you always dreamed was your father.

And in the hot days you lay opposite each other, unclothed and dripping, and in the cool days you wrapped yourselves in furs, locked arms, legs, hips, and now between you the great warmth. And inside this world you constructed there seemed no distinguishing the days from the nights, for you slept in the hours all others knew as the day, while during the night you made love and told stories and considered the possibilities of the world, for your great glory would soon follow. And when you woke to her weeping she looked upon you with red and fearful eyes, and when you spoke she said nothing, and when you touched her shoulder she left the tent.

And there were days when you held her, when you kissed her neck, her ears, and against the heat of your affection she talked of your child, how he would be as his father, how you would raise him into manhood. And she groaned when you said the Almighty's name, going to the opposite side of the tent and refusing to speak when you reminded her you would be called to minister. There she sulked, withholding her favors, until you said, "Perhaps I may seek some... reprieve." Now her eyes lit with a fire and she fell upon you in a fever.

And other days you went into the forest, into the deeper grasses, inspecting your traps for the stillness of a recent kill. Sometimes you returned with a deer or rabbit or squirrel bundled in dripping burlap, while other times you returned drained of color and scarcely able to speak. Now you murmured that the shadow of the creature floated over the trees, cackling in the voices of dying lambs. Your voice a delirious cadence until your wife turned away. "Please," she said. "No more of this." And you insisted, "I pleaded with Him. I kneeled before the mountain and I begged, 'Is it not enough that I conduct myself with righteousness as a husband and a father?'"

And you never confessed you sensed the presence of the natives, the flickering of their feathers, the glistening of their greased arms, the almost silence of their movements.

And the creature perched upon the hillside, watched your shadow make love to the shadow of your wife, saw you suckle from her, leave her red marked and moaning. And now the hunched, monstrous figure circled the tent, and in the morning the soot-burned tracks, the brimstone smell.

XXVIII. Your wife said nothing when you told her of the creature and she said nothing when the natives finally crept from the forest, their bodies painted gray and white and adorned with feathers. The grim pantomime they performed, elongated motions, and fingers pointing from their heads like horns. In silence you watched them, while your wife remained in the tent, and now her chattering teeth, and now a low, breathless sound.

Day into night, and when you told her of the natives, the shadows of their dance, she held your hand to her belly, whispering, "What would you tell him?" and now you were silent, and now you felt the heat beneath your hand, and you said, "To love all the inventions of the Almighty," and you knew then the corn silk softness of his dark hair, the lazy weight of his skull against your chest, the distant murmuring of his child's voice, and you said, "He will know his letters and he will know his numbers," and "I will tell him always to run in the grass, for a child is too young to toddle in the dust," and you continued with your instruction long after your wife fell to snoring. And through all the hours of the night the natives continued their tumult, ceasing only with the morning light.

At dawn their spears jutted from the horizon, while the fumes of what they cooked carried, pungent and wild. Your wife sniffed the air and cried that her child needed food. Now you opened your final tin of peaches, and your wife clawed for them, slurped them greedily, lips and hands glistening with syrup. And the child was not sated, and your wife moaned for the ravenous life within. Now you went to your traps, and here lay the shattered figure of a rabbit. The jut of native spears almost impossibly close across the grasses, the wild and incoherent language. Now you skinned and cooked the rabbit, and soon you wiped her greased face and she slept as you stroked her belly. Now you propped her head onto your lap, whispering that she fulfilled what no other could, and how all these years you had drifted but now you were happily moored in her arms. And then you placed your ear against her belly, and from within came no movement, no murmuring. And to this silence you whispered, "Sleep now, my dear little Isaac."

XXIX. In the morning you woke alone in the tent, and now you found your wife waddling in the snow-streaked fields. There she stooped and grunted and pulled at the stalks of brown grass. She gazed upon you with eyes pale and dead. To see her you almost could not move. Finally, you touched her shoulder, her hip, and in a voice choked you whispered, "The ground is frozen." She gazed beyond you, her hollow eyes, her cracked and bleeding lips, before she finally pleaded, "Will you try?" You brought her to the tent and covered her in blankets, and there she lay, feverish and shivering. Now you built a fire with the last of your cabin wood. Her wane visage in the flickering.

And when you said her name she did not stir. And when you repeated her name the sound emerged as a croak. Now you beat the ground and you seethed and you struck at the air, and you grabbed your skull, and you heaved, and you heaved. And now you left your wife, sleeping and shivering, yet slick with the heat of the fire and the terrible heat within, and you ventured across the grasses.

You meant to plead for herbs and medicine, to barter your very soul for their sacred insight, but when you reached the far grasses you found only the smears of dead fires, animal bones charred beyond edibility, the beaten-over places where they had danced and erected their tents.

And now within the forest you found no animals, and the cabins were emptied of their goods. And the ponds contained only the unbreakable gleam of ice. And had you found cows milling in the fields you would have returned with jugs of milk, and had you found nests in the trees you would have brought eggs. Instead, you heated lumps of snow, and with this you boiled your left boot, wrapping your blistered and bloodied foot in rags. When the leather softened you pried the leather from the sole and fed your wife the slices, and she sucked and supped upon these cutlets as if they were the finest veal.

And you have said you faced the black mountain, your brow pressed to the snow, whispering, "Please, do not forsake us." And you pledged further honesty and charity, but not your service, for your soul belonged in devotion to her alone. "O Father, she is all my heart, can't you know this?"

XXX. And that night you woke while she murmured to her belly. When you pressed your ear to the flatness she said, "Do you hear him sing? What a lovely melody there." And how could you admit you heard only silence? That you felt no movement? How could you say anything other than "Yes, he will be a lovely lad."

And in the night you boiled your other boot, the brown bubbling and the murky fumes of rot, while the eyes of the natives glowed through the trees. Their silent creep across the snowfields, while your wife gnawed and slurped.

And how many days did you ask the Almighty, "O Father, have I done wrong?"

And when the natives returned to their camp, their fires rose as shimmering walls, enclosing the sky with smoke, and their shadows bucked and convulsed. You pulled your sleeping wife against you, her belly and unconscious moans. The knife you clutched in wait.

And in the dawn the snow before your tent was crusted black with char.

And you awaited their assault, and when no assault came you awaited their emissary, and when no emissary came you cried, "He watches over us still!" but your wife noticed nothing. She slept against you, pale and sweating and murmuring, and now you rubbed her brow with a cloth made cool with snow, and whispered to her of all the days to come.

Then the snow clotted the sky and drifted thick against your tent. And the drums returned, the birdlike cries and rhythmic chants, and the fires flared and the snows melted. All the world became shadows and heat; vast, glowing ruins; the wife you held, covered in skins; your whispers, lost in the ancient din. And you told the child in her belly that you would protect him always. And the Almighty would watch over you three until the end of time. And perhaps in this moment you even believed your words.

XXXI. You woke alone, as a cold wind blew through the opened tent. Your wife lay before the tent, bloodied and nude from the waist down, lines of soot drawn across her throat, her chest, while her eyes flickered with a child's simplicity and confusion. Her clothing slashed away and cast to the snow. You gathered her into your arms and you did not scream and you did not sob. Inside the tent you wrapped her in blankets and skins. And she cried for her child, so you returned to the snows, and there the cord, shriveled and cut away, coiled in the red-soaked snow. There you dug until your hands numbed, raw and blood dripping. And you saw no bloody tracks of man or animal. And no wailing cry did you hear, and no child did you find.

Now you ran without guidance from the mountain or pause for prayers. Through a world vast with snow you ran, and you ran beyond your endurance for pain, until your feet numbed and your arms seemed as stone, and then your body simply stopped, and you fell to the snow and there you lay, unmoving, and everywhere seemed the sound of her screams.

Your wife's father found you beside the road, purpled and frost covered, rouged with the blood of your wife and what you believed was the blood of your child. He found you murmuring in a language he could not comprehend, and some have said you were found uttering in tongues.

XXXII. They warmed you before the fireplace. In your fever you told them the Almighty's creature had come with black wings flapping. And the mother and father merely looked at each other, and then the mother draped moist rags across your brow and the father, the butcher, threw a glass against the wall. He would have strangled you had the mother not stood before him. And so the father left, and while the mother paced you lay, babbling in your fever.

When you woke, you staggered finally to the room where you once stayed, and with a voice feeble you cursed the day you first heard His name. But even then you smelled the brimstone of the creature's trail, and the windows did seem to glower with its light.

And finally the butcher returned on horseback, your wife, pale and sagging against her father, bound to him with twine. You waited, mute in the shadows, while the butcher shouted at his wife, and now the two rushed back and forth with rags and steaming bowls. So they cleaned her numb, shivering body, water basins soon blood murky, and then they piled her with blankets and coats. And then they waited to know.

How many nights did you hold her in her convalescence? How many nights did she cower beneath the pale sheets? And now lucid you denied to the mother and father any mountain-sent creature had come. And when your wife began to speak of what she had seen, you said, "No, no, my darling. It was natives. In your heart, you know, they came from the forests." And you told her the story of the tragedy in place of the one she recalled.

XXXIII. So it was the butcher and his wife had lost all of their children but this wife of yours. And had you asked, he would have led you to the white stones where they lay beneath dust and loam. And in the blue glow of the falling sun, the butcher lit his pipe and gestured to the mountain. "That god of yours gave us a terrible road to travel," he said. "Please, never again take her from us." He could not look at you, or you at him, and finally in a voice wavering you promised you would not.

After some years your wife again conceived, and soon this child toddled in the dust. Fallen often in those hours onto his stumpy knees, his face transformed into redness and wailing, and how quick to hold him, to soothe, was your wife. The child's face clasped to her breast and muffled and calmed. How strange to not leave him in the dirt, for such lessons alone you had known. The butcher, a playmate unto your child as he grew, chased after the boy, growling with outstretched arms, while your wife watched and laughed. And in these hours you stood in the shadows, watching while the butcher tended to your son.

In the evenings your wife read to the boy, giggling as if she were a child herself. And as he chased butterflies along the breeze, she gathered him into her arms, spun him, his arms and legs ever outward. And there were hours when she dozed with him, amidst the long grasses and the yellow flowers, while the foxes and barn cats came to watch, fleeing at the sign of her waking. And when you were home you stood behind the house, listening to the sounds of their play. And you closed your eyes and considered the days of your life that had led to this moment.

And when your wife asked why you never held your son you stooped to the child, who pulled away, wailing. And you said it was for the gathering flies that the child seemed wary, for now you worked alongside the butcher, a butcher yourself, ever spattered with blood and offal. You said, "I could have washed better, perhaps." And you clucked your tongue to the boy, as one does to chickens, and still the child drew no nearer to you, merely clasped his arms about his mother's legs, sunk there into her dress. And you went to pet the child, as one does a cat, and again the child wailed and wept. So it was you retired into the house, and there you sank to your knees, repeating the name of the Almighty a thousand times over, begging Him to remain on His mountain.

And there was no room for the Almighty within the butcher's shop, not His words or symbols upon the walls, nor His voice in the skulls and the bones, the spatter and the gristle. Yet the Almighty taught you patience and the Almighty gave you skill, until even the butcher marveled at how easily you hacked meat and bone, and gesturing to his shop, its flies and tables, he said, "All of this will someday belong to you." And it is said you felt only gladness, for you understood the language of the meat. You knew the story told by the curves of the red flesh, the lines, as well as any illustration in any book, the life lived and ended so that some man and his family could prosper and fatten.

And in the twilight of those evenings you departed into torch-lit streets—the butcher by way of his carriage while you insisted always upon a stroll. And the dung stink, the moonlight glow in the slop. And you listened to louts congregated outside taverns, no longer engaging with these men. Now the mountain alone held your attention. Some nights in the open air, you lingered in the streets, the dirt roads, waiting for some gesture. And when the voice of the creature nowhere sounded you said, "I do not wish to be a great man—just this man." And you said through gritted teeth, "She is my only glory. The boy is my glory—I want no other." And you said, "Your silence has given me joy." Now each night you returned ever later, ever wearier, and your wife said you seemed as if you had seen a terror. You replied, "No, I've seen nothing at all."

XXXIV.

Now one night a voice came to you in a dream. And it sounded in a compulsion deeper than sense, and now you were drawn across the land, and now you walked through the birch forest, where the bark flaked like strips of skin and the suicides smiled with bloody teeth. The rocks steamed and a terrible wind moaned at the foot of the mountain, and you ascended, and the sky shone with the vastness of the universe, the immeasurable darkness everywhere burning. The hours and days fell to ash. At the peak you waited, and in the dirt a blade and a bundle of kindling. Now from the darkness a voice droned in the sound of trumpets, "One does not become a shepherd of men without the payment of blood." Into the din you cried, "Father, I brought no lamb." And the voice replied, "So I will gather my own."

XXXV.

Soon you and the butcher constructed a small home across the tall grasses from their land. And there was a room for the child, and there was a room for you and your wife, and there was a room for all of you to sit in community. And so it was your family grew by two children, a daughter and a second son. And your children ran and played in the dust of the yard. And they petted dogs wandering the roads. And both daughter and son carried wriggling barn kittens in the skirts of their dresses, held open into hammocks. And when the children fell into illness you said the name of the Almighty, and when they rose healthy you said the name of the Almighty. And you were not yet thirty when your temples grayed, when your expression lined and cracked, when you first saw the world as through a thin gauze. And, yes, your wife sagged at her shoulders, her breasts, but none would say she did not remain a beauty. None could say she did not arrest your heart when you saw her at common tasks—the stirring of a stew, the hanging of the wash—or when she stood in silence in the bedroom, oblivious to your gaze, her curves beneath the loose fabric of her gown. And how gray she seemed in the dawn, asleep and painfully fragile. After all the years, she remained all you knew and all you wanted to know.

And most days you thought nothing of the Almighty or His creature. And to ask your wife she would have said the same.

XXXVI. Yet some days your wife woke speaking the name intended for your first son. And some afternoons in town she inspected the faces of pale native boys, or the faces of woodsy boys drifting through town or leaning on fences, those with black hair and eyes as brown as her own. And she sought those young men who darted along the streets, dusty and barefooted, wild with tobacco and liquor. Ever you restrained her—"It is not he"—and ever she disappeared into you with each such revelation. But when you were not with her she searched the streets without limit, calling in a hoarse voice the name she never gave the child, a name never discussed but within the forests of her dreams, the ache along her heart.

XXXVII. And the night your first daughter fell to fever, your wife tended to her with rag and bucket. The child slow choked of life while she gazed and pleaded with her eyes. And you dabbed at her brow and you held that still, cold hand, and rather than say the name of the Almighty you said, "Oh, my girl. Oh, my sweet princess." And when the child forever stilled a sob tore your wife's breast, while in their beds your other children wondered if they would see their sister again. And to them you soothed, "Someday, yes, a long, long while from now." This assertion punctuated by your wife's cries, while her mother pulled her from your daughter, who slid limp across the bed. How small a life is in the mind of the Almighty. And the butcher breathed heavily at your side: "You must be strong for your family." Only now you realized you held a bottle of your wife's cooking sherry, and you set this aside. "Oh, yes," you murmured to the butcher. "Of course."

And only in the years to follow did you say that on this night you heard the creature's claws clatter upon the roof.

And when your second son fell to fever you laughed maniacally, and you told incomprehensible jokes during the prayers the priest led the others in. And you pulled away from the butcher as he took you from the room. He called your name and you babbled and spat. And you said the names you called your child, and you said the moments when you had loved your child best, and these fell into the open air a derangement of language and tears. And with rubbery legs you went into the dust of the yard, into the moonlight, and there you knelt. And you said you would burn all the flesh of the butcher's shop as an offering. And you said to the shadow of His black mountain, "Please do not kill my son." And you said the given name of your eldest boy, and you said, "Please do not murder my Isaac."

Only now did the lip of the forest shine with a horrid light. Only now did the awful winds bid you enter.

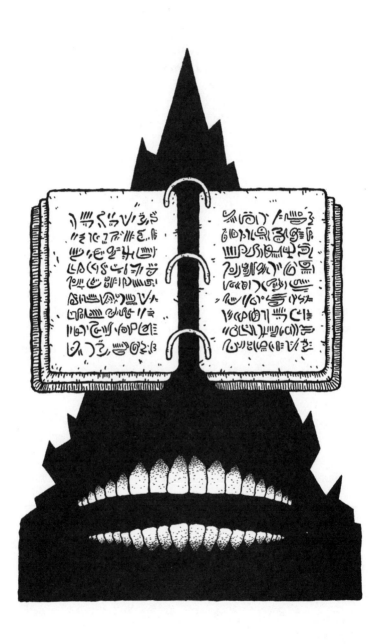

BOOK II
WIDOWS & SONS

I. You returned to find wife and son and the butcher and his wife before the open grave of your second son. You were hued black with soil and your clothes seemed as rags, your jacket held before you in a bundle, but rather than ask of your condition your family gasped with fright, for your eyes glowed with a lively madness.

II. And in the first days of what you called your "ministry" you removed a stack of golden plates from beneath your jacket, and you set these golden plates into a burlap sack, and you tied the sack with twine, and you set the sack in the dankest closet in your house, and you padlocked the door and about your neck you wore the only key. And there you left those plates to sit and molder. And when your wife asked why you locked the closet you explained, "For no reason at all." And how often you woke to the Almighty's creature swaying alongside your bed, its wings and the bony hooks protruding from its wings. And when you cried with your hand upraised, "Please, but one more week!" your wife awoke beside you and she saw no creature, nor did she scent its atmosphere, the faintest lingering of brimstone.

And when you found your boy standing before the closet with wide brown eyes and trembling lips you shouted, "Isaac!" and you seized his arm and swatted him upon the rump, and the boy wailed and wept, and as he fled the room you called after him to never again stand before the door.

And as you ate, and as you bathed, and as you rode to the butcher shop, and as you sliced fat-mottled flesh from bone, and as you laughed at the butcher's jokes, and as you wrapped the chops and the loins and the ribs and the kidneys like glistening loaves and the livers and the jowls and the noses and the hooves and any other requested cut of meat, and as you wiped the gristle from your hands unto the fly-strewn towel, and as you walked the black night, and as you gazed unto the mountain while holding back the sickness, and as you continued into your house, and as you removed your clothes and stepped into your flannel pajamas, and as you lowered yourself against your wife, snoring or murmuring of the children she had birthed only to see die, you heard only the hum of those golden plates, the rustling of the Almighty's creature along your floorboards, and through the blood crashing in your ears, the thumping of the veins within your neck, the coarse, furious pulse of your heart, you knew Him upon His black mountain, ever and ever again uttering your name into the faint and terrified reaches of your soul: *Joseph, Joseph, Joseph, Joseph, Joseph, Joseph, Joseph, Joseph, Joseph, Joseph.*

III. And you have said you knelt in the yard, whispering, "The language is meaningless to me, a mystery," and pleading, "I am not the instrument you seek." And you have said you soon discovered a pair of wire-rimmed glasses on your nightstand. These glasses seemed as ancient as the plates themselves, although they were neither cracked nor dusty, and you understood then their purpose and their origin. And to hold them seemed to place your entire figure within a vise.

And when your boy stood in the doorway you saw him through these lenses. There he seemed a bulge of coal, or a char, or some awful, scorched thing. You flung up your hands, crying out, "Be gone, Evil One!"

IV. Soon the morning came when you told your wife the Almighty had finally chained you fast to the wheel of your "terrible duty." She said nothing, her eyes wide. Now you fell to your knees, weeping, and her hands fast within your hands, as you cried, "Oh, my darling, His heart is so very full of love," and by this you meant, "Even if we fled He would find us. No corner could seclude us and no fish's belly could shield us."

You led her into the room you called your "office." There your desk stood swept free of debris save a jar of ink, a crow feather quill, and a stack of loose paper. Now you said, "None but I may see these plates," and your wife said, "Plates?" and you said, "We must bring His Word to the gentiles." And she seemed frozen when you bade her "sit," and "take up the quill," and "listen well," for your ministry depended upon her faithful transcription. And when she did not speak or move you led her by the hand, lowering her to the chair with a gentle pressing of the shoulder while into her hand you thrust the quill. Finally she whispered your name so softly it seemed phrased as "?" and you replied, "I will be nearby," and in the smallest voice she said, "Where?" and when you did not answer she asked again, "Where will you be?" and now you said, "Within the closet." And so you went.

And you have said that within the darkness was born all the hues of light. And from your lips came the sounds and words of the Almighty's ministers, the paradise they sought and the lands they pillaged. And you spoke of the doom they found: dead and decaying on the beach, their armored garments rusting and tinted golden under the light of a falling sun, the tide lapping through moldering sockets, and the jut of spears, and the motion of shadows, and the howling of what others have called devils or savages, but now you understood as the lost progenitors of all humanity. And from your lips to your wife's fingers to the pages before her. How soon her fingers seemed as black as oblivion while the pages of your ministry rose in columns. How she wept for her hand, bent and crippled, and ever the cracking of knuckles, ever her gasps, soft and terrible, and still you did not pause, for the language fell continuous and irrepressible once you traversed the depth of the void.

And you continued without respite through the night and into the next day, pausing not for food or for drink, and when your voice broke and hoarsened your wife transcribed words like "cough" and "wheeze" and "rasping." And when your boy stood in the doorway wanting dinner, his mother could say only, "There are potatoes to be boiled," and "You know what to do with a chicken," while from the closet came the strangled rasping of his father.

After some fifty pages were translated you emerged, hollow faced and pale, the hair fleeing your skull in wild shocks and your bloodshot eyes rocking back and forth. Your voice rasped some incomprehensible language, and you gestured for your wife to lay down her quill. How she gazed at you. And when you had fed and rested you said, "We must bring these pages to the gentiles." And you laid your hand upon your son, saying, "Your father has been called into the ministry," and you said, "And so you also have been called into service," and when he asked, "By whom?" so it was you answered, "By the Almighty, whose terrible word is all."

V. And so you selected the most pertinent of these pages, those that read "The light is the spirit of the Almighty," and "When the old people heard any blasphemies of His name they tore the blasphemer to pieces," and "Justice calls aloud for an infinite punishment of their sins," and "We are placed here, in the midst of a glorious sensible scene of visible things, a world that is truly amiable and beautiful, and may be said to be the image of the Almighty," and these pages your wife and son copied a hundred times over, while you paced and gesticulated and raved. Thus you issued the Almighty's new commandments, for you needed not the creature to usher forth His commands— now the words simply appeared in your mind as if they were your own thoughts.

VI. Now before your first mission you led a lamb into the yard, but when your son saw the lamb's kind eyes and the blade's cruel glint he wept and fell before the beast. And you could not pry him away. And the boy pleaded. And he wept and wept and he cried, "Oh, Papa, then you must kill me!" So you bargained with the creature, immense and terrible and issuing char with its very laughter, and finally the creature uttered a new proclamation in its awful language. So to your son and this lamb you returned, and this lamb you pardoned with great booming show, claiming the Almighty had decreed the end to all burnt offerings, for all men now stood as lambs of God.

VII. And you commanded your son to place the loose pages of your ministry into the hands of the towns-people, so he went about saying, "Behold, the new words of the Almighty." And stray dogs trotted in his wake and birds over-burdened the trees, watching him by the hundreds. But most citizens he came upon furrowed their brows and sent your son on his way.

And when they mocked your son's claims now you went door-to-door, smiling and preaching and glad-handing. And when your wife asked to be absented from these excursions you commanded her to walk at your side. And so she went, whispering how she felt naked before the eyes of all, saying, "I did not know it would be like this." And by this you figured she meant the wife of a great man and prophet. So to her you insisted, "It will become easier. You will see." What a fine presentation you both made, she in her finest blue dress with her red shawl and feather-trimmed bonnet and ink-blackened hands, while you stood in your soot-black coat, your high collar, and with the onion-slender pages you outheld as you announced, "Brothers and sisters, the Almighty has blessed me with His terrible presence."

And the servant girls who opened the doors gasped at your eyes, bloodshot and rocking, and you learned to insert your boot into the entry, saying, "I am here by commandment of the Almighty." And when the lady of the house came you said, "Madam, I am here to speak about the Almighty." Her pale, severe face as she said, "Aren't you the butcher?"

And very often you were led into these homes, and very often the children stood silent in their velvet jackets or sailor outfits or their dresses, and perhaps the husband sat puffing his pipe, and perhaps he sat in the library with a glass of whisky, and perhaps he sat on the back porch, gazing at his lawn, or his yard of dust and chickens, or perhaps the small woods he called his, for many a man in those days longed to survey the bounty of which he was master after those hours when he was made to know the smallness of his life and power.

And sometimes the husband commanded you leave, for he was already "too much put-upon" by "maniacs" in his regular hours. And sometimes he allowed you your say. Now you cleared your throat, and the words to follow surely originated from His lips. And sometimes the husband offered you a drink and smoke, for you were known as a "joyful fellow," and always you declined after your wife glared. And sometimes the husband and wife listened to your language, and sometimes the entire family gathered, and sometimes the smell of woodsmoke, and sometimes the glow of oil lamps, and sometimes the flicker of candlelight, and sometimes you waved a book you said was filled with your "revelations" but was in fact an empty ledger. And sometimes their eyes glazed while you revelated, when you said, "Rebuke the tempter and punish the sin," and "The inward actings of Grace are invisible to others," and "Let people be friends and helpers to their own welfare," and "I propose to my brethren to drop the use of the elements and the claim of authority in the administration of the ordinance." And if your audience drifted in their attention, you clapped your hands and said, "Consider now what you desire most and the Almighty will whisper in my ear the substance of this desire." And in a voice booming you continued: "Yes, my friends, He will bequeath me the power to fulfill this desire." And there were those who closed their eyes as if this would invoke the power you described, and there were those who said, "Perhaps some other evening." And some offered you a lamb and a dagger as if you required bloodshed, and unto these you said, "He has decreed no more shall we murder the meek." And now you brought the family onto the front lawn, promising to "conjure his language." So a liquor was poured onto the readiest bush and now a lit match was dropped. How the leaves and limbs blossomed into flame. And before the bush you crouched, mock-whispering to the blaze, "Speak your secrets."

And you said the flames from "ancient times" had served to convey messages from the mountain unto the intelligence of "even the humblest fellow."

And when you were not cast out you revealed what the ash and smoke said: "You desire most that those you love will never die." And no man could contradict these words, nor could his wife, nor his children. And now you said, "Salvation is found only in the light of the Almighty, and the Almighty is found only through the language of my ministry."

And maybe only now were you cast out by the boot of the husband, or the hee-haw laughter of the husband, or by the muzzle of the husband's musket, or the wife's weeping, or the screams of the children as their yard flickered and glowed with the embers of their shrubbery.

VIII. Soon those who believed your revelations wise and true gathered before your home. And so you held up your ledger, saying, "The sun, moon, and stars have had more worshippers than the uncreated fountain of light from which they derive their luster," and "There is a difference between having an opinion that the Almighty is holy and gracious and having a sense of the loveliness and beauty of that holiness and grace," and, finally, "We have in great measure forgotten our errand into the wilderness." And these followers lingered in the dust of your yard and they trailed you to the butcher's shop, loitering there until the butcher tossed them into the street. And when the butcher asked who these people were you told him of the plates you kept within a box, covered in burlap, and hid within your home.

And the butcher asked, "Have I not been as a father to you? And unto your children?" You said he had. And the butcher said, "Why then would you not tell me any of this? Why would you not warn me of what you intended to bring into our lives?" You began to say, "Because the Almighty commanded it so," but when you saw his fallen expression you said, "I do not know." And when the butcher sighed, you reached for his shoulder, saying, "I did not think to do so." And the butcher soon departed in silence.

And your followers loitered your yard through the failure of the sun. They stood as smudges of darkness along the edges. They built bonfires and cooked venison and rabbits, but when a lamb was brought for slaughter your son stood before them, crying out that offerings had been outlawed. So you nodded that the boy was correct. "He no more requires such sustenance," you said.

Later, the butcher returned, shooting a musket into the weeds, so now your followers fled to the outer shadows of the yard. Now the butcher's eyes gleamed a terrible light, but when you relented not his posture sagged, and with a voice anguished he sighed. "Do you hate me so much?" he said.

"I hate no one," you said. "A preacher has only love for the world, my dear butcher."

Now the butcher demanded to see the plates, and you revealed the Almighty's decree that none but you could look upon them. But little strength you had for his tears and gnashing—you brought the butcher to your house, and onto the kitchen table you set the plates, covered in burlap, with great noise and ceremony.

"This is them?" said the farmer.

"Indeed—these are the golden plates of the Almighty's testament," you said. "See how they glow."

He shook his head. "I see only burlap."

"Some glow protrudes," you said. "There and there—you see now, yes?"

"I see nothing. Pull aside the cover."

"The Almighty has decreed—"

"Goddamn your Almighty!"

Silence.

The butcher wept. And he wailed: "To do this to me—after I have been as a father to you—"

"—I have only one father—"

"—and gave you land to raise your family."

"All of this is His land!" you shouted. "What you see here and what you cannot see. From a thousand feet below the soil to the peak of yon black mountain—all of this is His, butcher, and all of this He has decreed as inheritance to my ministry."

Now upon his knees, whimpering: "Just show me the plates—"

Proudly now, strutting as a cock struts: "You may place your hand on the burlap covering, but you may not look upon the plates."

"I gave you my daughter—"

With pity now: "This is for your safety, don't you see? These plates would annihilate you. The Almighty's light is not for mortal eyes."

IX. Now strangers approached you on the streets, from the shadows, asking to hold and look upon your plates, and when in a high, exalted voice you insisted none but you could know their holy glow these strangers spat: "Don't forget who your friends are, fellow." And some, smelling of moonshine, grabbed your coat until you wrested free, and others pressed you into corners with jagged bottles and pipes to slit your throat and smash your skull, while no one ever heeded your cries, while ever around you the world continued with its commotions and its machinations.

Soon even your journey home proved treacherous, for bandits lurked in the darkness, beneath trees with pistols and knives, wanting nothing more than the glory of your plates and the fortune they would certainly bring.

And thieves slunk about your farm, watched your family through spyglasses, and at night they crept across the yard, hunched silhouettes in the moonlight, peered in the windows, and in the morning the many smudges of their noses marked the glass. Soon even your ceiling creaked at night as they crawled about your rooftop on hands and knees until you brought them down with a musket fired to the sky. How your wife and son wept for these intrusions. How they begged you to return those plates to whence you found them. And some said you now hid the plates in the loose hay of barns, or in the shadows of lofts, or in the dankest corners of caves, or beneath the moldered leaves of the forest. And others said these rumors were of your dispersion, insisting you stored the plates where you always had, although these too had multiple theories about where exactly in your house the plates lay, for your wife and son dared utter your story to no one.

X. As the infamy of your claims spread, more pilgrims and wanderers and empty spirits and dreamers emerged from the roads. On the dust of the yard they constructed patchwork tents of deer hide and quilts, and around fires they gathered and chatted, their faces weather blistered and gaunt, their long, yellowing beards. And you chatted and joked with these men as if you had known them all your life, although in the early days your father-in-law scampered after them, musket drawn, until he pulled up gasping for air. They wandered the edges with spirit-ravenous eyes, and when the butcher quitted his terrorizations they resumed their posture on the yard. And your wife peered through the kitchen window, a musket at her side, while your son attended to his chores. When you found her thus you bellowed for all to hear: "Put aside your weapon, my wife. The Almighty has brought these gentiles and the Almighty will have what the Almighty will have." And from her place by the window your wife did wonder, "Why are you shouting?"

Evenings you went unto your flock, playing cards and swapping stories of your devotion to the Almighty, and indicating their tents you said you knew such structures well. And some say your visage shown with the deepest sorrow when you said, "For in such places I have long lived, and in such places I have suffered for love."

And you asked, "Brothers, why have you come to me?" And some said they had always known an emptiness, and some said they feared death above all else, and some said a dream brought them, and some said your humble, unrefined manner called them forth, while others attested to the compelling nature of your story. And some men said the Almighty's voice approached them in their lowest moments, and now these men spoke of their mortal doubts and afflictions, and, yes, they confessed unto you their frailties and what secret horrors they dreamed at night. And a man named Samuel explained he had forsaken his daughter and wife to hang in the forest of birches. "Such was my mysterious sorrow," Samuel said. "All my life, this terrible emptiness." He had removed his watch and shoes and composed a note of farewell, and this note he had nailed to a tree. But at the final moment a voice came to him, saying, "No, you shall not."

And now as one they feasted, gnawed rabbit meat from spindly bones and tore hunks of blue-spotted bread, and when they had no food your wife brought them soup, and they slurped this oily broth, although what her trembling hands did not spill was often cooled and greasy. And as they ate you hunkered in the shadows, and then finally in the quietest sounds, you wondered what should be done with His new pilgrims.

XI. Mostly now you did not work at all. Through the days customers and busybodies told the butcher they had seen you ministering to the sick and crippled in the streets, and others found you wandering back roads, gesticulating to the heavens, and still others indicated you remained with your pilgrims, and there you passed the day joking and playing cards.

And such a morning came when the butcher declared, "Either you clear this rabble for good or I have to fire you. My God, son, I will have to evict you. Don't you see that I will banish you from your family if you don't shake free of this madness?" Gravely you nodded: "I will speak to them now." So you went unto your faithful, and when you found them, snoring near the faded embers, you called for them to awake. Now they sat upright, rubbing their eyes, while you said, "My brothers, He has come to me in a dream. And there He decreed we will build a great church and there we will preach the word of revelation." And when they asked where you would build this church, you answered, "The Almighty will guide our hand."

And when they asked, "When?" you answered, "When our translation is complete," for you and your wife worked through most days, her hands now gnarled and ever blackened, no matter how she washed and scrubbed her flesh to bloodiness. How she wept to see the quill and ink, set before her. How she trembled to hear your voice, echoing from cloistered rooms.

XII. Soon strange eyes populated your followers, and now black-whiskered men stood on tree stumps loudly questioning how "a butcher's apprentice, clearly unschooled," could read such an ancient script. "It is unreadable with the naked eye," you answered, pulling the glasses from your pocket, and you explained they contained "a great magic." You said for any other man these glasses would work only as a typical pair, clarifying the natural restrictions of sight, and you said, "In days now long distant, many of you knew my skill with the seer's stone. Many of you know the power bequeathed me by the Almighty and the riches I once gathered. This is much the same." And when a great many of these followers sought to question you further, you waved them quiet: "For now you must have faith, for the Almighty insists upon it. In time you will witness a great many wonders, for our Father intends to return us to Paradise."

XIII. And one morning the butcher approached while you stood amongst your followers, saying, "I have hired a fellow to take your place at the shop." The way he spoke you would have thought his entire family had perished, this man whose whiskers shone entirely white, his hair thinned to wisps. "My good man, it is understood," you said, touching his shoulder. "My worries now are of that mountain"—you gestured to the smote blackness—"and the ancient fellow who lives upon it." The butcher's stricken expression as he sagged into his clothes, drifted the outskirts of your camp as a mere and fragile spirit. And he spoke unto you no more for the rest of his days, but many nights he was said to speak of you in his dreams. And some said by midnight you had forgotten his name. And some said you had never known it.

XIV. And while you dressed for sleep in nightcap and gown, your wife lay in bed with wide eyes, listening to these crowds' hymns heard vividly on the wind. "Husband," she wondered finally, "when will they disperse?" And so unto her you laughed: "Why, my blossom, not until the end of time!"

And when she asked why her father would no more meet with your family you simply looked at her.

XV. After some period of toil a man arrived at the encampment with hat in hand. All were stopped for the finery of his dress, the gentleness of his voice, and how he paused at the head of the walk to smile at the song of a jay. Once in your home he stooped for the ceilings, and when he dwarfed your chairs he crouched pleasantly upon a stool. His calm, simple smile.

"The Almighty has visited me," this man said, his bland, gentle tone.

"Has He?"

"Yes." He nodded. "He told me of the marvelous work we will accomplish."

(*Your raised brows.*)

"I am to help with your book—"

Interrupting: "How very interesting, because I have received no—"

But already this man continued with his story. He began before the beginning, with his father's ambitions: come from distant shores to tame the wild by force of will. And he described his father's sad end, the old man gone from "oaken figure" to "a collection of mere sticks," and unable to eat or drink the fellow passed on to the mountain with scarcely a rattle. They wrapped this frailty in linen and laid him to rest beneath a slender willow. "For the first of my life I stood fatherless and alone, although I stood in the midst of a great many." Vigorously you nodded: "Yes, I know of these matters." And this man continued: "And then I was told all the land before me and to the reaches of my imagination was mine, and so ever after, my wife and I have lived surrounded by a great plenty of barren fields. You see, our abundant land has been overgrown from disuse." You were silent, considering, and then, "Where is this land?" and when he answered you nodded deeply.

And the creature ever watchful fogged the windows with his blast-char.

So this man was named Martin, although others called him Harris, and still others deny his existence as a phantom or some madness similar. No matter.

XVI. And that night, while your wife feigned sleep, you said unto her, "The Almighty long ago promised me He would send assistance in a man's figure. I had forgotten. But that man has now arrived." And into your wife's silence, you continued: "You will be pleased to know I no longer require your help in transcribing." When she still said nothing you asked, "Did my wife not hear me?"

Only now did she whisper: "Yes, my husband."

XVII. And Harris occasionally cried out, "His foul hand is at work!" while he labored, and when you emerged from your closet you found him cowering in the corner or standing on the table, because a page had shifted, or a candle had blown out, for Harris believed the Evil One's machinations everywhere present in mundane doings. How much effort you expended insisting the Almighty would allow no harm done to those who furthered His designs.

And how Harris moaned when your wife observed him at his occupation, how he covered over his eyes, closed the door and propped a chair there. And so never again was she allowed to see the text or hear the language, and never more did you invite her on your "missions" into town, for now you brought Harris alone. And you admonished her when she wept. And when she said, "I do not trust this man—I have heard queer stories about him," you bulged the wall in with your fist.

And when you rested in your labors there was lemonade sometimes outside your door. And sometimes you drank and told Harris someday when this work was finished you would hike to the black mountain and together gaze upon its splendor. And this good man wept with simple joy.

XVIII. Now wherever your wife went she listened to the encampment swell, its joyful song and murmuring prayers carried on the breeze. And in this group there were those you had charged with planning the construction of the church, although your wife did not know, so when she watched them through the kitchen window, hunched over unfurled papers, pointing branches here and there, gesticulating with some passion or fury, she believed them plotting some terrible strangeness. She watched warily until the day she could observe them no more, and now she went to where there were no windows, and there she sat, watching the walls in silence.

So you found her one day, and to her you loudly said, "My dove sings no more." And when she responded not you leaned to her, and repeated your saying. Slowly from the wall she turned, and now she merely looked at you.

"The flute—" you said quietly. "You no more play the flute."

Now she regarded you with a powerful blankness.

"You used to play the flute, didn't you?"

Through her teeth she sighed. "Yes, my husband. I once played the flute."

XIX. And that night, as their fires glowed through the bedroom windows, you said, "There is much doubt ripened within your heart." When your wife denied this you said, "I have insisted that He must be patient, that your faith will grow, but He insists it will not be so." And now you took her hand, your voice breaking, for her tears were apparent in the light of the fires, and you said, "Please, you must open your heart. Oh, my wife, I beg of you." She watched the yellowed glass, the shadows flickering, while in a frenzy now came their songs about the Almighty's creature. You pulled her hair aside, your fingers across her cheek, and she gave you no other notice. How long then before you went to your closet, and sat before those plates, ever shining?

XX. As word of your church grew, many gentiles arrived in wagons with pitchforks clasped, looking for your plates, asking your pilgrims why they followed a man on his word alone. Your followers answered that they trusted you as "an actual man," and by this they meant you were in no way schooled or educated or warped by the vanities of life, for you had struggled in the dust and the offal like the rest. And when no others could corroborate the existence of your plates, when not even your wife, or your son, or the butcher could speak with certainty of their existence, there were some who spoke of "opening up that house" to see for themselves. And there were those who said "this is nothing torches and guns" could not sort out. And soon a man you did not know rapped at your door, telling your son to fetch you "before we burn this damn building to the soil." How your child came to you in tears, babbling of the mob. When you stood before this man, stinking and bleary eyed and some weeks unshaved, he said with his mouth of darkness and rot, "This is your last warning before we take what is ours."

And when you returned to the house the creature stood within, smoldering and glowing red. And when it opened its mouth the creature yawned a terrible fire, and so you were made to know the way of its path.

XXI. And in the glow of their fires, and in the shadow of their shovels and guns, you told Harris the Almighty had revealed a new mission. Now you copied out a dozen holy symbols, and giving him this scroll you said, "You shall be the steward of this ancient script." So you bade him journey to a university of your naming. There he would bestow the scroll unto a professor of "antique languages" who would grant the symbols his certificate of legitimacy. But when you announced Harris's mission your gathered people said, "You send the man who speaks to animals?" for who had not witnessed Harris's communications with a squirrel or deer he believed to be the Almighty. And you said, "I send nobody unless He first commands it."

And indeed Harris met with the professor in his office of dust and books. And there are those who say this professor marveled over the ancient script, soon issuing a certificate. And there are those who say he translated the scroll to read

"And there shall come a man of the lineage of Joseph who will return His true word to all the land," but after Harris explained the origin of the plates, the professor destroyed the certificate, shouting, "There is no ministry of angels!" And there are those who say the professor "guffawed himself red and tearful" before proclaiming the language to be "insensible squiggles" and "mere stupid illustrations of plants and animals." And there are those who insist the professor told Harris, "I worry over you, man," for he was convinced your "plates" were little more than a confidence game. And indeed he wrote letters to the gentile papers decrying your texts, but only after you had long perished from the earth.

And the news of authentication was cheered greatly within your yard and derided as "lies" and "hogwash" by those who chose to disbelieve the word of the Almighty. But very few followers left the encampments, and much of the turmoil subsided, for indeed in Harris's absence you had returned to hunkering in the camp, telling jokes and playing cards, and you promised that the Almighty would allow those of "the strongest faith" to see the plates soon enough.

XXII. And now you returned to your book with a renewed vigor—Harris's fingers dusky with ink, his expression haggard and worn to the nubbin, for you worked this man some fourteen hours a day. And while his penmanship was not as elegant as your wife's, nor was his spelling so accurate or his punctuation as proper, none could ever doubt his enthusiasm for the work, for he arrived earlier than even you, his quill and ink and paper readied when you entered the room, and none could question his belief nor his earnestness, for he never wondered of what you saw in the darkness, nor did he express concern at any scripture you shouted, no matter how crazed it sounded, although there were moments he could not suppress his wonder and delight, muttering, "Marvelous," and "Astonishing."

And when others asked if he hungered even slightly to see the plates, Harris said, "No, I don't believe so," for often he had already known their radiance in dreams and visitations, and indeed he had there been promised to know them in person when "the time was at hand."

XXIII. In this time your son grew and developed, and soon he wearied of standing in your doorway or trailing at your heel, of never hearing your praise or even the commonest expression of devotion or love or interest, for no more did you throw back and forth some ball, or read to him stories from his various books, or even say his name or look upon him with anything but an expression of surprise, and perhaps now you would say, "Oh! You!" as if only now remembering his existence. This son roamed the camp with absolute freedom, and soon he knew every follower's name, those established and newly settled alike. And he was a great favorite to all, for he carried no animosity within his heart, nor pretension in his manner, nor did he covet the goods of any other, and in fact gave his own to those who had little for themselves. And he listened to all, never joking, but smiling at the jokes of others. And when some animal ventured to the yard he often tamed the beast. Yes, your boy passed many hours in the sunlit dust, stroking a feral squirrel or rabbit, and to this creature no harm would come, for none could bear your child wounded for the slaughter of his little companion. And he was a great favorite of all the children, for he allowed himself abused by the older boys and he wrestled the young ones with tenderness.

And he was often seen walking in the long grasses or strolling into the forest with the freckled daughter of the follower known as Samuel, and there they rested on a log, watching frogs and dragonflies, clasping hands in uncertain mutual silence. How at night she feigned sleep alongside her mother and her father, before crawling into the moonlight at your son's signal, the hooting of an owl or the tapping of a woodpecker or the pawing of a barnyard cat. They went into the forest, where they traded the language of their affection, and there they were said to lay with each other, although most called this only a posture of sleep, believing they were too young to do any other. And there were those who said Samuel woke one night to her absence, and peering through the opened skin of his tent he saw the slither of her tracks. And there were those who said he took his pistol to the forest with impulse murderous, but when he saw your son's figure upon his daughter he set his weapon aside, and he returned to the tent without word.

XXIV. When Samuel ventured to speak of the friendship between his daughter and your son, you did not answer the door, nor did Harris, nor did your wife. And there were those who advised Samuel that the friendship would bring favor to his name and there were those who said you would excommunicate him if you knew. And none admitted he feared you could do worse. Soon your child spent his hours at Samuel's elbow, and he sat for dinner with that family, and never again would he sit with your own.

Soon your son revealed to Samuel and the others that the Almighty had commanded him to take Samuel's daughter as his bride. And when the boy ventured to your presence you were moaning with your brow upon the kitchen table. And now he called you "Father." And he proclaimed himself a man, and now you finally saw him before you. "How old are you now?" you asked. When the boy said his age you smiled: "Is that so?" And he insisted on helping with the plates, for "if you have this in you then I must too." And you answered, "There will be time enough for that, Isaac"—and the boy began to say his name was not Isaac—"for the Almighty has decreed that you will follow me as head of this church." This was tabulated within your ledger and would be revealed "when right." And with this announced you again settled your brow against the table. For a long while you heard no sound, and when you looked up the boy was gone.

XXV. Little you saw of wife and child in the following weeks. To see the boy meant you gazed out the window and to see your wife meant it was dinner, although you now seldom dined; most nights now, your wife sat alone in the candle glow, with beef and potatoes and carrots plated for three. And perhaps she consumed these foods with plodding bites and stared at the wall, the table, her hands. And perhaps she could eat nothing at all.

XXVI. So continued your days until Harris came to you, wild eyed and clasping a letter from his wife, where she called the professor's endorsement "hardly satisfying," for this wife was a great skeptic. Now Harris beat his head with his fists until blood streaked his brow.

"My fellow," you cried, "what is it?"

"She means to leave me—"

"Is that all it—"

"—if not for some proof of our labors."

You clasped his shoulder. "Buck up, and to hellfire with the weaker species, man!"

"She will leave if I do not bring the manuscript." And he tore his hair in bloody shocks. "Oh, I will die without her!"

Now when calmed you asked Harris of this wife. And from around his neck he drew a gold locket, saying, "There sits my wife, as she has looked in years past." So this woman in a blue dress, her blond hair tied up, her blue eyes faint in the miniature, and indicating her neck you said, "Is this mark true to her likeness?" And Harris said, "Mark?" And you said, "Does she wear a black mark upon her neck?" and he said, "Ah. Yes. She does. She has always." And you regarded her some while before you said, "I will see what we can do about this troubling matter."

So you consulted the Almighty in the depth of your closet, the creature there snorting and scrapping and unfurling its wings within the confines, for the mortal limits of space and time fall aside for a beast of the Lord. Finally you emerged, saying, "You will take the pages of our translation, but no one must know of your journey. And you will show these pages to no one but this wife. And you will return immediately after you have shown her." How the camp murmured as Harris departed, calling after him to no reply.

And as his figure diminished to the distance you watched the creature follow after like some immense burned vulture blotting the horizon. And when both had diminished you realized for the first in a long while you smelled nothing of brimstone or fires.

XXVII. And now your wife found the door to your room open, and you alone within, and no papers sat before you, nor ink, nor quill, and when she asked, "May I come in?" you smiled: "Of course, my love, why not?" And when she laced her arms about your neck you did not pull back, and when she kissed your cheek your hands found her hands, and now into your ear she exhaled: "Oh, my husband, has it ended?" And to this you laughed. And to this you said, "Oh no, my wife, all of this has only begun." Now she fled the room and you found her weeping in some distant corner.

Your hand now at her shoulder. "Have faith, my darling," you said. "If not in me then in the Almighty. And if not in the Almighty then in me." Now your hand against her cheek, and there such softness as you spoke: "Has He not already blessed us with this lifetime together?"

That night you both lay in the folds of your bed, and now she whispered, "Hold me close as you once did, husband." You turned to her, your body warm into hers, and now for the first in a long while you lay together as man and woman. So you came to know the distance between the girl you had wed and the woman you now held, and how strange she felt, for the body you had known seemed gone to dust, and the movement of your hands seemed the inspection of a woman entirely new, and the beauty of this woman was the bounty of her figure, curved in ways the girl never was. Such is the fever when it overcomes even a man of the Almighty: soon you were lost in the tasting of her neck and the devouring of her chin and lips, there opened and welcoming. And her taste was a new taste. And the having of her was a new occupation, for she no longer lay beneath you as in your days in the tent, fixed and unmoving, screwed up and terrified of what duty demanded, but now she moved against you, now she grabbed and sucked, and now she chewed, and now she dragged and bucked her pelvis, and now she pressed herself into your mouth, and as you tasted her now she tasted you, and as you pushed into her now she moaned. Now she rent your flesh and the blood sang in the air.

And in the soft light of the morning how gray and figureless was the woman before you. And when she turned over, her eyes tender, smiling, uttering your name with a tone of affection, you looked away, saying, "Up with you, then, for there is much work to attend to."

Through the window your wife watched you with the ladies of the camp: how they laughed and blushed at your jokes, how natural you made the touch of an elbow or the brush against a cheek. And she commented not when you went to her at night, when you peeled away her clothing, when you fell her across the bed, those wide brown eyes. And now you counted the freckles upon her chest, described them as constellations, gave them new names in place of the old. And in these moments of endearment the childish mystery of old was cast aside for the entirety of years past, and all the days you had known each other, and all the days to follow. And how sorrowful and lonesome was this lovemaking on the ashes of the worlds you had built, only to see them dead and cast away.

XXVIII. And while you awaited Harris's return so it was the belly of the girl your son tarried with began to bulge, and soon your son announced to you, "We are to marry." You gazed at him for some while before saying, "Who?" He indicated the girl at camp with her parents, their anxious glances from the fire. And you said, "No doubt she's very lovely," although she had not bathed in weeks and her face was clouded with smoke and ash, her figure engulfed by garments loose and bulky. "But loveliness fades—a woman grows husky, she becomes gray, she mounds and mounds. And this says nothing of what becomes of her character. For the love she shows you now she will someday show her brood alone." You sighed, wrapped your arm about him: "There is much alteration from the girl to the woman, my lad, so beware this one." And from your pocket you removed a locket, saying, "This was once your mother. You now understand how she has wilted." And the locket you held before you was Harris's own.

"But the Almighty has visited me—" the boy began.

"Has He now—" You smiled.

"—and He has—He has—He has ordained our union."

"Probably you dreamed all this."

"He appeared in a blinding light."

"I wonder why He told me nothing about it, my young sir." Now you patted the boy on the head, although he now stood near your height.

"We have learned from your own lips that the Almighty gives visitation to all." And the boy's chest seemed to expand as he spoke. "And from your own lips we have learned the Almighty will share His language with even the commonest fellow."

Now you put your finger to his chest, and how solid it was, how substantial, and there are those who insist you began to say, "Don't believe everything you hear," but instead you said, "Don't think I won't remember this, my young Isaac." And you said, "Then you will clear out of this home I built, won't you?" and you said, "If you're man enough to wed, you will lay with this girl under your own roof, as your father assuredly did and as your father's father most likely did."

Now the creature awaited you within the room in which you translated. And its eyes burned the smoke crimson. And some say you wept and beat its chest, and some say you wrestled the creature upon the floor, and it left your shirt in tatters and drew gashes along your chest. And some say it gave commands and you merely nodded.

And in bed that night you ran your finger along your wife's smooth girth, and you said, "I have been told the Almighty will grant us a new son in place of the old." And you said, "I have been told all of this will be his." How still she grew. How rigid and cold. And when no passionate entreaty was met with like passion, now into her ear you mewed: "My wife, be reasonable! The replacing of this current son is the Almighty's bidding, not mine."

XXIX. And your son went next to his grandfather, professing his desire for this girl. And the butcher only looked upon him to weep. Now the butcher's wife gave your son a package of salted bacon and a kiss upon his brow, before begging him to return home, for "a young boy's place is beside his father, no matter how strange."

And while your wife wept and pleaded your son gathered his schoolbooks and his trousers and his shirts and his jacket and his boots and the quilt and pillows from his bed. And from bedsheets and branches he fashioned a tent on the outskirts of the camp. And within this tent he lay with the girl as a man does with his wife, and he pressed his hands to her belly, and he felt the slow expansion as the life within struggled and kicked. And to her the boy said, "It knows it's me."

"Of course he does."

XXX. In many ways now your fever subsided, and you no more longed to rave within your closet. Such yearning for the greatness of His Word no more ravaged your soul, and through the day now you wandered your camp as a shepherd watches over his flock, stopping to tell bawdy jokes, offering advice on the card games they played. And when you returned to your wife in the night she believed you were again the man she had known before the days of your ministry. She saw not the creature uttering its language into your ear. And in the hours you scanned the horizon for Harris, your wife prayed no rider would approach. And so it was she prayed to the Almighty to curse that man, Harris, offering "any sacrifice no matter how mighty or trifling" to see him made no more. And when each night she closed her eyes your wife saw this man Harris cut apart by knives and ravaged by a thousand dogs, and she smiled to hear his screams.

XXXI. Then the evening came when a wailing was heard from the camp. Eventually Samuel neared with hat in hand, explaining his daughter was ill. "Lay your hands upon her," he pleaded. So you went into the camp, and there you found your followers massed with hats in hands, and expressions solemn and eyes downcast. And you peeled open the skin of the tent, and there the daughter, her wide-open eyes, glassy and unknowing. Beside her the mother crouched, a damp cloth pressed to the girl's brow while before her a red and clotted mass, unmoving and expressionless. And your son stood in the shadows, weeping not and expressing nothing through his ashen countenance. And the girl said no words. And she did not buckle, nor did she thrash. And so it was the wailing you had heard was from the mother, now mute and tearless. And you could not breathe. Now you went into the open yard, gasping. And when Samuel came to your side you moaned, "This girl is not ill—she is dead." How calm seemed the silence before he whispered, "You promised our children would not die." You looked at him and you could not speak. So you returned to the tent, one hand upon her brow and the other gripping the rags of her shirt, and you seethed: "Rise," and "Breathe," and "Move." And this girl did not exhale. And she did not buckle. And now her once-fevered skin only did cool.

And you went out of the camp and Samuel trailed in your wake. And soon your son stood before you, insensible and sobbing, until you bade him fetch you a shovel. And you meant to wrap your arms about him and sob his name and say, "Oh, my boy, I have known this pain," but instead you told him, "Such a time comes when a man may see some invention of his flesh returned to the soil." And to Samuel you said, "The Almighty giveth and the Almighty taketh away." And he again said, "You promised our children life forever," and you tried to explain to him, but instead you gestured to the black mountain, saying, "Your daughter lives with Him now." And this man argued no more. And no more did he weep or allow his wife to weep. And so it was he bade your son to bring another shovel, and he wrapped his daughter and his grandchild in cloth, and together your son and Samuel dug the graves. They returned to their tents in the evening, covered in the same dirt and streaked with much the same sweat. And so it was from that day forth your son called Samuel "Father." And your son called the wife of Samuel "my other mother."

When you returned to the porch your wife opened the door the slightest crack, asking through that barely space, "Why are you so pale?" and "Why are you shaking?" and you said, "I cannot say," and when the door remained open you insisted, "It is no business of ours," and when the door yet remained open you finally admitted, "Our son is healthy and alive." Now the door closed. And you did not go to her; this night instead you remained alone, thinking of your first days together on the plain, and the ways you each suffered in the shadows.

XXXII. A day soon followed when a speck showed on the line of the horizon, and how quickly you saddled your horse to meet this apparition. And you rode faster when you saw the creature circling in the clouds above. And you called out, "Goddamn you, Harris!" until you saw the stranger who approached, his face dust blackened, a leather satchel slung over his shoulder. "You are that revelator?" he asked, bringing from his satchel a letter writ in Harris's hand and addressed to "the revelator." It was not written in lemon juice nor was it composed in code. And you cursed Harris's name.

The letter began with recollections of the weather, of his wife's appearance when he first arrived home, the way she read the pages in silence, the chicken and potatoes their cook roasted for dinner, how they ate in mostly silence. And he mentioned encounters with old acquaintances, the drinks they shared at the tavern, their kind inquiries of "my recent activities." And so it was Harris told them of the plates. And Harris told them of the translation. And Harris told them where he kept the translation. "Sadly," his note continued, "I realize too late how I have acted in error." And you cursed his name, and your hands shook and your teeth chattered and you fell to your knees, weeping. And at your choked commandment the rider read the rest aloud: how Harris returned to find the mud spatter of boots through the parlor, and up the stairs, and into the bedroom, and there "the dresser wherein the pages were kept was dismantled and clothing and drawers strewn." And so the pages of your translation were gone. "We are looking for them," Harris concluded, "seeking out the thieves. This is why you have not heard from me in the weeks since our designated hour."

XXXIII. And you rode through the day and into the night, the creature circling and blotting the sky, the sound of rage throbbing your veins, until you found his property. His yard was a rolling hillside, and the house seemed more like a courthouse or capitol building or castle than any house you had known. And his wife stood in nightgown and shawl, a candle in hand, before the open door. She was nothing like the woman in the portrait. And you two gazed at each other until finally she said, "He is not at home." You staggered past, calling his name, and from room to room you went, brandishing your riding crop, until you found him in his nightcap and gown, squirming under his bed, his bare legs and feet protruding, and you cried out, "You have damned us all!" His swinish cries while you hauled him from the bed. And the creature beat its wings and you thrashed Harris, the blood droplets leaping from his hands, the back of his head, until finally his wife shouted, "Stop this!" Now you let the crop fall to the floor. "You have damned us!" you wept before all.

You took over his office, and there you smoked his good tobacco and fumed, and when in the days to follow Harris came to seek your forgiveness you said, "Brother Martin, it is not my forgiveness you need seek," and you gestured to the black mountain, saying, "Don't you know what He will do to us?" and you said, "My word, man, we will roast in eternal fires if we don't find those pages." Now you sought the streets for the men Harris claimed he had spoken to, and when Harris could not recollect their names nor their appearance beyond their "spectacles" and "whiskers," you said, "What do you know of her whereabouts at the time of this theft?" and you leaned in close, saying, "What do you know of *her* heart, Brother Martin?"

XXXIV. Those pages were never found. Finally Harris announced, "I will commit any penance to see our slate made clean." And the creature whispered in your ear and so foul was the brimstone you nearly sneezed. Then you announced His verdict: "You are to bequeath your home and all of the land surrounding your home unto..." and you began to say "me" but you corrected yourself: "... our church." And Harris opened his mouth, and then he closed his mouth, and then he said, "If that is the Almighty's desire."

And when Harris told his wife of his penance she shattered dishes until the air fogged with the dust of porcelain, and the floor streaked with her blood. You found her in the kitchen wrapping her split hand, the black-red-soaked bandage. Your hand to this wound as you asked, "I wonder, good woman, if you know the whereabouts of those pages?" How she cried out when your fingers tightened.

And that night the creature showed to you the ways of your coming greatness.

XXXV. And soon the land beyond what was once Harris's yard was filled with the familiar tents and smoke and stink, the dung and flies, horses and mules, and the lines of wash buckling in the breeze. And you walked this new camp as a general does, swaggering and calling out, "Some fine land here, eh, boys?" And you began each morning by calling out: "Look sharp, fellows," or "Boys, listen up," and typically you followed with some speech on the nature of the Almighty's glory. Now, however, you told them, "We must begin our temple." And so the men cut and hauled pines through the grasses—the echo of their labor, their calls of "timber," their arms and hands sticky with sap, the fires they built coughing green and black fumes.

As you surveyed the work, Harris ventured to your side.

"She won't even look at me," he said.

"My dear brother," you said with a sigh, "we're fortunate He did not cast us into the fires."

"She calls you a wicked man."

"What does your heart say?" you implored. "What does the Almighty tell you?" For you often found him speaking in hushed, reverential tones to sparrows and dogs, believing His voice manifest in these beasts.

Now no more did he question your glory to your face.

XXXVI. And your wife could not suppress her wide smile as you led her through this house. And when she asked of her parents you said, "You are nearly thirty, my darling—it is time to cast off our youths." And she did not weep or argue, for she saw there were more and more rooms, silk-upholstered sofas, splendid golden-framed portraits of persons unknown, statues of naked children with wings and muscular men wrestling bulls. And touching a clock taller than she, your wife said, "Who knew there were all of these things in the world?" And in the room you called her "recital room" she found a baby grand piano, and how she held you, her kisses and warm, streaming tears. And later, after she ministered to your needs, your wife wondered, "How will I ever keep this house tidy?" and when you said you knew nothing of those matters, she nodded: "Surely I will need a servant girl or two," and so you decreed this would be arranged. And now she slept on a spring mattress with down pillows, so soft all her aches and miseries seemed diminished to none. And while she dozed that first night you regaled her with stories of the Almighty. And when she rose on that first morning she began to say, "All my faith is in you now," before she caught herself, saying instead, "All my faith is in Him."

XXXVII. And you and Harris translated in his old library, taking breaks now to sample the cognac he had squirreled away, the excellent tobacco you each puffed to daydreams of an expedition to the mountain, while outdoors ever continued the chopping of his pines, the milling of timber with long saws, the continuous labor of men who were bankers and farmers and shopkeepers and schoolteachers before they were born anew in the Almighty's light. Their sleeves rolled to their elbows or these men shirtless entire, their grunts and exhalations with the back-and-forth thrust of the long saw, the flex and ripple of their arms, the pinched red expressions, these men made blond by the shavings and dust of pines, caught on the wind and mounded in the fields.

And when you returned to the manuscript you explained to Harris, "The Almighty has said the stolen pages will return manipulated and cloaked in misinformation to cast doubt upon His word."

"Yes, yes." Harris nodded. "Some creeping beast has told me similar."

And so it was you would not begin at the beginning. Rather, you would begin where you left off, summarizing the first pages of your book within this new book to "counter the machinations of the wicked." Now you worked with a mere bedsheet suspended between you, and Harris later claimed he "witnessed the celestial glint through the sheets, and the hunched shadow of the revelator." And when asked if the creature was ever apparent, Harris replied, "Creature?"

XXXVIII. And while you labored at your task your congregation labored at theirs, the pounding of nails, the sawing of boards, the erecting of structures, until one wall was hoisted, and then another, and soon men populated the rafters, walking and hunkering upon them, chewing tobacco and observing the world below. There they worked while wives and daughters watched anxiously from laundry lines, or from wells, pumping water into wooden buckets, and there the men rested, the frenzied rise and fall of their chests, and there they told rude jokes no woman or child would admit to hearing. And in the evenings you wandered the rafters, crouched with your men, told the same blue jokes they told. And when you apologized for the "old habits" of your sinful past they praised you as a "right down-to-earth preacher." And when you said, "Well, I never was much for education," many of these men confessed that neither were they, while others said, "Were I not, so I could act by the goodness of my heart alone." And so it was you knew these men would follow you always.

And now your wife was a helpmeet to all the camp, no more the quiet and downcast of eyes, for now she carried herself "as a lady," her head held erect and her bosom out puffed. Now at her instruction all the wives and the daughters of the camp brought tins of cornbread and buckets of water to the men while they rested. And your wife carried water and bread to your son, who ate his lunch alongside Samuel. And the two sipped from the same ladle. And they ate from the same plate. And in the evening they sat before the same fire and supped from the same pot. And your wife spoke kindly and softly to Samuel, blushing as she talked, while to her son she said, "Your father would appreciate seeing you again." In a sullen manner the boy replied, "I'm here, am I not?" And when the women were not cooking or washing you sent word through your wife that the women must till those soils long fallow. Now these women, stooped and dusty browed, scattered seeds while your wife oversaw beneath a parasol, and while the men laid the floors, and the men hammered the walls, and you drank cognac and translated your book with a man who spoke to birds and wilted before shadows he considered of wicked intent.

XXXIX. And you and Harris worked busily, until your voice hoarsened, or Harris's hand numbed beyond feeling. And from the grasses below Harris's wife watched the shadows of your figures playing off the walls. And often Harris left you snoring on the floor, although some evenings you remained awake long enough to visit with your wife, who updated you on the progress and the mood of the camp, calling the gardens "flourishing" and the temple "breathtaking." And when she spoke of your son or some mood or ailment of her own, you interrupted her with the stories you had translated that day. "How the world will tremble before these revelations," you said.

XL. The evening you proclaimed the book of your ministry complete, the men of the congregation arrived at your porch with torches and shovels, asking to see the plates, for "we have lived in fields of mud and constructed a temple with our bare hands for this book." And now the boldest stepped forward and then another, until you cried out, "He will cast you into the flames! He will cast us all!" They hesitated before one shouted, "He's bluffing!" And now you went into the house, and there the room expanded with ancient darkness, and the creature seethed and hissed and the light of its eyes glowed like lanterns lost in a sooty fog. And when you returned, you gestured to a man in a brimmed hat and to a man with long white whiskers and to a young man with wide, searching eyes. "You are the chosen," you said.

Now Harris whispered in your ear: "And me as well?"

"You are indeed a tragic figure." You chuckled grandly for all to hear.

Now his back straightened. "This was my house," he said.

(*Silence.*)

"How will you publish your book without my money?" Now you again consulted with the creature, before returning with the decree that Harris could "join in."

XLI. Once in the woods, you shrouded your face, screaming that a light dissolved your hands and peeled open your lids, and that overhead the creature flapped its terrible wings and yawned flames. These men cast silent glances until one cried, "I see it!" and another said, "Oh my!" and the third admitted, "It is beautiful! And terrifying!" When Harris alone saw not your creature, you smiled. "Brother Martin prefers the spectacle of squirrels," you said. So Harris journeyed into the darkest reaches of the forest, and there he prayed before the swinging shadows of suicides. When he returned he fell weeping for the creature's terrible beauty, and now when you shouted, "You see it holds the golden plates!" each of the others reached with struggling fingers.

And the creature told these men if they testified to the brilliance and authenticity of your word as the word of the Almighty, they would be named "elders of the new ministry." So they assented. And when one asked, "Can we not keep the plates in our temple?" the creature replied, "There is no need, for the earthly task is accomplished."

And when the creature fled in a burst of light you cried out, "He is gone!" and so it was there remained no scorched smell of atmosphere, nor glinting gold of plates. And all in camp agreed you and your followers seemed as those who had experienced a "hallowed state," for your eyes were glassy and your hair arranged in mad shocks. Now you gathered your flock, saying, "Boys, we have spoken to the creature," and in this way you introduced the men as elders. There came some applause and some murmuring, and when one woman said, "But there was to be no priests," you replied, "Who is your husband again?" Now when her husband stepped forward you asked if he wished to question the Almighty, and this meek, trembling follower scuffed the dirt with his bootheel. "No," he said. "Of course not."

XLII. When the temple stood as finished you walked the silent aisles, pressed your brow to the floors, whispered to the boards. Now at the pulpit you gazed into that room's emptiness and spoke words hallowed and now forgotten. And when you lifted your hands, the silent ghost of your fingers and palms remained.

Now the women of the camp filled wooden tubs with well water, nude but for their knickers, dabbing themselves with sodden rags and fatty bars of what they called "soap." And the men bathed in the nearby river, naked and shameless before the Almighty, laughing and sudsing up and retelling your most outrageous jokes, for there was a great joy in the coming of the Word. Thus cleansed and straightened, the men shaved for the first in months, all now dressed in the finest clothes they retained from former times, the women with their peacock-plumed hats when they had them or their hair up when they did not.

And in the hours before service you did not compose a sermon, nor did you wonder of the substance of the sermon, nor did you consult the books upon your shelves or the book of your composition. No, in your solitude you simply came to know those words you must speak.

From the pulpit you saw the world of your construction, the multitudes now seated and expectant, and none of them knew you as "the orphan boy." And to your wife you looked, and to Harris, and to your son, seated with Samuel and his wife, and now to those who waited through these moments of hesitation and silence. Now with the first cracking of your voice in this cavern of a room, you said the Almighty had visited you, that you had journeyed to His mountain and there you had known all of the valley below, and He had said, "This world is for you and those you love." And He said, "You will be known by all as a man of revelation." And He said, "There will be no gatekeepers, for all men carry divinity within." And He said, "All men shall stand as priests." And He said, "The names of women will be cast to the dust." And He said, "They will be known as Wife or Sister or Daughter or Mother." And He said, "And she will stand as a helpmeet to her priests, to her brothers and fathers, and to her husband before them all." And it was said you puffed your chest, growing into another man, strutting as a cock struts. And all spoke of your eyes, fevered and wild, and all seemed possessed in their grip, and indeed many wept and leapt to their feet, crying out "Hosanna!" and many fell, raving in tongues and thrashing in exaltation. And when they woke they remembered only the love and power of His embrace.

After service many fell at your feet, and you said, "Rise up, brother, for no man shall ever again belong at the feet of another." How flushed you were, glowing with His power. How your heart pulsed. How you said, "We must expand our coffers," and then you corrected yourself, saying, "Congregation."

XLIII. Now you traveled from town to town in a donkey cart illustrated with paintings of you clasping the plates, crouched beneath the tremendous horror of the creature, and you walked door-to-door in a new top hat, black waistcoat, high-collared white shirt. And sometimes your wife journeyed with you, and sometimes you found your son with Samuel. And when he would not come along you took him roughly by the scruff, and now sullen and silent he joined you door-to-door. And you preached that you followed the way of the Almighty "for the eternal welfare of my son, whom I cherish more than my own existence." And when the boy refused to praise your church you cuffed him as you ambled to the next house. And you proclaimed the era of smoke and blood and offerings truly gone, and you iterated that this would be an era of love and tithing. And you proclaimed houses would be built, for no more would your congregation molder in the dirt. And you proclaimed the publication of your book. And you ordered the skins and heads of lions, and you hung these in your library, your parlor, over your bed, and there the impressive shadow was cast, and often you were found, lost in thought, gazing at their frozen snarls. And you explained, "Someday, when the coffers allow, I will import them live, and they will fill this house with their roaring." Now expenses only increased: traveling salesmen exhibited rare papyrus scrolls you absolutely needed, and you and your wife and ministers required many new garments, and your wife desired dishes to replace those destroyed, and it was said soon one temple would not be enough. And the bottom of Harris's funds was surely nearing. So you doubled all tithes.

And to the boys too young to work you proclaimed, "Jobs are everywhere!" and soon they swept floors and cleaned streets and worked on farms and in factories and mills. And you proclaimed, "Labor builds a character you will someday need, for each of you lads will become a priest, and you will tend to your own spiritual flock, and you will need to know what it means to suffer under the rule of another." And those men who already had work were compelled to find more, and those who labored only on your land now opened bakeries and shops, and those who sang or fiddled gave performances in town squares. And all men to some industry, for all men must tithe in what you called a "marvelous harmony."

And as the cash heaped into hats and baskets, you wept, saying, "See how He smiles from His mountain at your devotion and sacrifice." And many women wished to work at jobs in town and to them you said, "Tend to your children," and when they said, "Our children are grown," or when they said, "We have none," you said, "The Almighty commands you and your priest make some," and when they said, "I have no husband," you said, "A woman without a man is as a cart without a wheel or a horse without legs." And you touched their elbow or their shoulder or their chin, and you said, "Come now to my office and we will discuss this matter further," and you led them inside, where it was said you "discussed eligible bachelors."

XLIV. And when your coffers swelled you ordered the first printing of your book. And soon volumes arrived, crated and stacked in a wagon, and deposited onto the dust of your yard. And the children ran from their tents. And the women ceased their knitting, or their darning, or their washing, or their cooking, or their weeding. And now you bade some lovely blue-eyed daughter to fetch your wife. And while you split open a crate children swarmed and strewed packing straw to the wind. And copies were passed from woman to woman and all marveled at the heft. How many young ladies now came to you, saying with admiration, "You translated all of this?" And they smiled, batting their eyes, until your wife attended to the scene with her quiet, dignified air. And now those ladies returned to their chores, while you said to your wife, "My darling, I owe all of this to you." She smiled, saying, "Do you? Really?" and you asserted that you did, but when she opened the book you laughed: "How curious is my dove!"

And when the priests returned from their labors you dispensed the literature of your new ministry and bid them study well. Soon all stooped, reading and exclaiming at the revelations within. And the night was populated with the noise of fathers reading to their children while their wives listened at the door. And so it was they learned of how holy men in armor and plumes had journeyed to these lands in centuries past, and so too had wicked men. And so the war between these wandering tribes had thrown both the wicked and the good under the pall of terrible ignorance. And in the absence of the Almighty the world had been given over to drink, gambling, fornication, false idols. "The stain of the gentile hordes," you commented, "is thick upon the land."

And you walked amongst them, saying nothing, nodding and suppressing a grin at the adulation of your audience, for how you swelled when they wept or cried out or turned a page with insatiable swiftness. How you said with hands raised, even when none said otherwise, "Thank you, but I was merely the conduit."

XLV. And now you made missionaries of all wives and daughters and sons, and these went forth with your book. And unto all who exhibited genuine interest they bestowed a copy of your text, and now many missionaries returned with strangers who immediately constructed their own tents. So it was your congregation swelled with strangers wandering, constructing tents, tithing reluctantly.

And houses were purchased and houses were constructed. And soon your yard was emptied of tents and mud and horses. Now all of what you called the "neighborhood" belonged to the men of your church. How fine it was to wander cobble-paved roads without fearing to meet an unruly gentile. And while the men labored so you could extract your tithes, the women tilled your gardens, and they cooked and washed and darned and knitted, and with much pride now in this time you said, "The quality of a community may be measured by the sweat of its laboring women." How you enjoyed the house-to-house stroll, taking tea and joking in the parlors with wives and daughters. And when their husbands and fathers returned from their labors, these ladies spoke only of "our dear Revelator," the coarse wit of your jokes, the way your eyes twinkled in the light, the righteousness of your posture.

XLVI. From the pulpit you tore the gentile gauze from the eyes of all. And you preached of the sins and follies of the world, and you preached of the godliness of man. And all swooned before your uneducated passion. And many fell to the floor shaking and foaming and speaking in tongues. And many rose to their feet with cries of "Hosanna! Hosanna!" Now your priests were asked to sermonize, and so they rose and raved at the gentile's vice, the harlotry of his ladies, the "wayward nature" of his youths. They claimed his lands were overrun by the "pestilence of sin," and they said such a pestilence must be "eradicated" if mankind were to survive, while from your chair you cried "Hosanna!" and all cried "Hosanna!" after you.

And you preached, "Best is the woman who is silent," and "Woman, stand close to your man, praise his ways, and nurture his spirit, for he is your priest, and your fortunes are hitched to his."

And with these preachings your wife ceased to attend service, nor would she speak to you or look upon you or grant you the favors owed to all husbands. And you prayed hard on the matter, receiving finally a vision instructing her to choose the hymns for your services. And through her bedroom door she said, "Choose?" and you said, "Perhaps you should compose one or two as well." And if she pleased the Almighty, someday she may compose a hymnal of her own. Now she rose from her room and prepared you a breakfast of bacon and eggs and hotcakes. And all were astonished and gratified by the sight of your wife finally toiling in the kitchen. And so it was from that day forth your wife labored always to make your favor, outworking even the servant girls, cooking only the foods you desired, dedicating her every energy to darning and washing clothes and plucking weeds from the garden. And when you returned home she dropped her tasks to massage your shoulders, to coo into your ear, and when you complained of a stiffness in your feet she removed your boots and massaged those soles. And when you said your nerves were frayed she fetched your pipe, your tobacco, your matches, and a glass of brandy. And she attended all your sermons, crying "Hosanna!" the loudest. And her selection of hymns was praised by all for their grace and piety, including "My Faith Looks Up to Thee" and "The Spacious Firmament on High" and "Work for the Night Is Coming." Indeed, her former airs were soon forgotten, and now all agreed your wife was the fulfillment of the female in the eyes of the Almighty.

XLVII.

Each evening you walked along the avenues of what you called "our town," and you watched the houses of your congregation, the smoke from the chimneys, the shadows moving within. How distant the mud fields must have seemed. How long ago the farmyards. And some nights you found cripples in the mud and vagrants roaming the dirt roads, and to these you bequeathed a new testament until they crawled away or spat on you. And some nights you walked to the boundary of your settlement before returning home. And some nights you continued until you came to a clearing and there a lake, the moonlight flickering on the black water. Here you sat in the silence, and reflected on what you had built and the world to come.

So there followed a night when you met a man in the clearing, hunched in the shadows before his fire. He called a man's name into his cupped hands, and you knew his voice well, echoing along the years. And your hands shook with ancient loathing. And your throat tightened with sick and madness for this man who knew what you had been. And your teeth rattled. And from the hammering of your heart came all the sounds of eternity. And you asked the Almighty to make hard your emotions and guide now your hand. Now the moon was obscured by the immense darkness of the creature, and so the beast's ancient language pulsed within your blood. And from the soil now you took a rock, and in the stink of the soil was the origin of life, and in the loamy musk was the decay of father and mother and child, and the future decay of wife, and your own foul dust to come. And you crept to the farmer. How ancient and gray, how easy to cave in and smash, to render into timelessness. Now he turned to you, pulling aside his hat, and in the light of the fire he said, "I know you." From your hand the stone fell, and now a second man approached from the lake, a bucket swinging from his hand, the doomed thump of fish within. And this man proved identical to the man before you. Men of your age, stout men of haunted gaze. And they ignored the rock fallen. And they ignored your eyes, crazed and livened. And the seated man said, "You're that preacher, so called?" Vaguely now you nodded. "We were coming to see you, Preacher," the seated one said, and smiled.

And now you thought to flee, and now you dreamed to retrieve the rock, and now you longed to summon the creature's great horror and gnashing. Instead you whispered, "Were you?"

"Yes, Preacher," they said. "We surely were." And now they told their tale of woe: Their father was a righteous man and a devoted farmer who one night did not return home. How the "creditors lined the road" and the family farm was lost. How the mother soon followed him to the grave while the brothers then devoted their night hours to the taverns and slept under the stars—

And you said, "What of the boy?" and they said, "There was no boy." Words spoken with certainty. And they smiled to look upon your fallen expression. And your vision seemed to cloud, and you settled to the dirt, while the brothers watched you. And you mumbled, "Wasn't there some boy?" And the seated brother smiled. And the other brother said, "We were the boys." Finally, the seated brother said, "Once, long ago, there was an orphan who lived in the barn, but he died of a fever years before." And you saw the dead pale face in the hay. And you heard the animals below. And you felt the body carried through the yard. You shook your head: "No, not him then."

And the creature shifted in the night. And its red eyes glowed.

"Our sister, however," one brother said, and you blushed and coughed and looked away. *"Your sister,"* you said. They quieted and looked at you, and you motioned for them to carry on. Finally, they continued. "Our sister," one said, "by then was married. We believed the husband to be a fine fellow, but soon he became known as a... as a man about town, and after some while..." And the brother's voice trailed, before resuming, "... ever after our beloved sister has lived on the mercy of ladies' societies. Such is our sad lot, Preacher."

And now you regarded these men, their rough postures and brooding shapes. All your days found in the silence of this moment. And now you trembled to speak: "Come, join my church," you said. "And bring your sister. For my wife and the wives of the others will take her in as their own."

And these brothers were not surprised at the offer, for the Almighty had come to them in the night, foretelling this event. Now you three clasped hands in prayer, and now one brother fell to uttering in tongues. There on the ground he foamed and babbled and trespassed the void. And when he fell silent you commended him on these utterances, for having pried from the firmament "a most ancient sound." But when you asked the other to offer words he merely mumbled that he was not given to fine speaking. And you embraced them and called them each "brother." And you said, "Now you and all you love will live forever."

XLVIII. You returned at dawn, covered in dew and dust, and now you announced to whatever follower you met on the street that a family would join your cause, and to a woman at random you said, "You must sacrifice your home." And that night the brothers held a feast in their new home. And all sang and danced and stuffed themselves with roasted duck and venison, and even after the fiddler tired and slouched to a wall, many continued in their jubilee. How many couples fled to the lawn, barefoot now, falling into each other, in the shadows, the moist grass and smooth dirt. And days later the sister arrived, attired in a widow's black gown and veil. And to the vocal brother you asked, "On account of her husband's death?" He shrugged. "This is the first I have seen her in such garb." She pulled aside her veil as she emerged from the carriage. She was aged, full in the face, in the figure, but you knew her all the same. And when the other wives emerged, chattering and calling out their various greetings, you knew only the woman before you. Soon your wife pushed past, taking the sister's hand. "I am the Wife of Revelation," she said. "Welcome."

XLIX. In the days to follow, many priests—the young and the single and riotous, the longtime married whose eyes glazed when their wives or children spoke, the freshly married who lamented their newly figured "shackles"—gathered in the brothers' parlor, playing cards, telling jokes, clouding the air with smoke and streaking the floors brown with their spittle. How you avoided the commotion of this house as you walked the streets. How you crept past, lingered behind trees, spying on the windows for some shadow of the sister. Sometimes the brothers sighted you and called you in, and when you demurred they persisted: "Don't be a stick in the mud, Prophet!" Now, while the brothers laughed and joked and proclaimed their skills as gamblers and womanizers, you watched from the back shadows. And when the fathers of pretty girls were not in attendance the brothers spoke freely of growing curves, or the lascivious glances they believed forthcoming from the sisters of men not in attendance. And sometimes the men winked and said, "You give me a week and I'll have that ass in my bed." And men you had ever known to be faithful and good-hearted cried out, "Why bother taking her to bed? What're outhouses for?" And all fell to laughter and cackling. And you did not laugh. And you did not speak. Some later said you suppressed your humor, and some said you were "already nipped at the nuts," and when one of the brothers called out, "Why so silent, Preacher?" some of the men smiled at you. And perhaps you blushed, and perhaps you shrugged, and perhaps you feigned a yawn, and perhaps you said what you hoped was a joke, although in the presence of these brothers you never could find your voice.

And some nights these brothers pulled you aside, asking of certain women of the congregation: "How did So-and-So's wife taste?" or "I bet she's wild in the sack." When you pledged ignorance they laughed: "Boy, you are the funniest preacher I ever met." And other nights these brothers asked the men at their table if they feared "our preacher here." Did they lie awake, anxious over your laws, your decrees, and your priests smiled, and one said, "Why, Preacher here wouldn't hurt a lamb." And the brothers became quiet, saying, "You see?" and one brother said before all, "Were we in authority this fellow would lose a lip or an ear," and the other brother said, "Or a house," and both concluded, "Or a wife." Now from the shadows you said, "But you are not," and these brothers cupped hands to their ears, saying, "What was that?" They laughed until their faces purpled, until the whole house echoed and shook with guffaws, until you forced a chuckle from your own throat. And then they stopped.

L. And another night Harris chased a stray cat through the brothers' parlor, begging of it remission of some recent sin, and when he hunkered to the beast the brothers pelted him with lit cigars. And while the cat fled Harris yelped and cried for his flesh singed. Now the brothers hooted, and then all others followed into laugher. And it was said that you laughed the loudest.

So the next day Harris came to you, saying the Almighty had told him to trust not the ways of those brothers. "What do we need of them? Were we not following a righteous path before they came?" So it is said he went about telling this to a great many others too.

And when Harris disappeared into the woods only his wife worried of him. And when you told the brothers to seek him out they laughed: "Ask yonder cat where its friend is." So you alone went into the forest. Deep in the shadows you found him, clawed open and made a house to all manner of creeping things. You found him eyeless and lipless and mostly chest-less, leaves and soil kicked upon him, surrounded by the scattered tracks of various animals of the forest. Here also were the tracks of another man, but these you did not inspect, for you told yourself they were the work of the wind, or some hiker long ago—no matter the yellow eyes and smoldering lips that whispered otherwise from the heavens above. And you made him a shroud of leaves, and now finally you covered him with your jacket. And you did not weep. And you said no words but words unheard and asking forgiveness.

So you told his wife that you found him praying to the squirrels, and from them he received a mission westward. Such was his simple faith. So his wife wept, and she called you a "thief" and a "murderer," and at dawn she was gone, never to return.

LI. Now you proposed an expedition to the black mountain, with the brothers and those elders who could be spared from work.

Your elders loaded packs with tarpaulins and poles and jerky and bread and canteens heavy with water, while you carried along your book and your ledger and a pencil. And in the evenings you sat before a fire while the brothers drank from a flask, and their eyes swam and they jeered at the others, the mountain, the Almighty, and the Almighty's Word. So the elders watched you say nothing to what the brothers spoke.

And one day along the road you asked a brother about the orphan who had lived with his family. "You said he died—were you just saying that?" And the brother smiled: "Am I the one who tells stories, Preacher?"

And when you reached the mountain the brothers insisted on scaling to the peak. Now you alone refused to climb, for many had fallen before the terrible light of the Almighty. "It is not our time to ascend," you said. So they went without you, and you watched as they went into the mist. And in the evening you built a fire and jotted into the emptiness of your ledger. And for three such days you waited. And no voice in the silence came. Finally they shambled down the mountain, slurring and bloodshot and covered in black dust.

"Did you see anything?" came your voice.

"He must not have been home, Preacher," one of the brothers answered, and now his fellow climbers smiled with dazed merriment.

LII. During this period came many of your greatest revelations. And when He bade you preach, you bade your wife clang bells until all the wives and children and priests emerged from their dwellings. And dinners went uneaten—plates pushed away, the flies alone feeding. And the studies of children too went undone; indeed all chores and hobbies and obligations were nothing against their obligation to the Almighty and His Preacher. And they thronged the streets at your summons, little boys darting in circles, mothers calling for them not to tumble in the dirt, while little girls skipped in velvet jackets and skirts. And some children sang hymns and some wives and priests joined hands and sang along. And all songs ceased when they neared the temple, silent but for the tittering of children as they filed into their seats. Finally the brothers and their sister filed into the back row, she dressed in mourning, her eyes averted.

You called this temple the "House of Revelation," for here the veil of dream was cast aside. And within this temple any earthly name you held was cast to the wind, for here the Revelator alone remained. And while you preached, and as you sermonized, women swooned and men raved and children sweated, eyes bulging and hearts thundering, and many nights these children woke screaming the name of His creature. How many children dreamed this beast in the whirlwind, the howl of flame. How many dreamed himself or herself whisked through the air by rough beating wings, their dream-throats hoarse and broken. And when passing carriages heard this jubilee as if from on high the travelers crossed themselves, or they entered the temple, and soon they too fell under your sway.

And you preached the narrative of your book, how those "original peoples" came in ships from distant lands, dressed in golden armor with horsehair plumes. They went in search of wealth and lost their souls. They became as savage as animals. Now they wandered, darkened by the fires, in ignorance of His Word, cast out of Paradise and drifting. How their souls screamed in agony from the fiery pits for this ignorance, although they were by birthright "His chosen people." And at first you preached how judgment could not come until the last of these natives were eradicated. And then it was your wife who took you aside, debating the point, and soon you insisted the natives be brought before you and converted into "soldiers of light."

And you preached the Almighty was once a man of "flesh and beard," who "walked the land on two legs," eating "the foods a man eats," drinking "what a man drinks," and tasting "the fruits of woman as a man tastes." And He knew the sorrows of the heart and He knew the anguish of existence, for He was born of dust as a man is born of dust and He returned to the dust as a man returns to the dust, but He ascended to the top of the black mountain and was born anew in a transcendent light. And you preached, "You and all you love will ascend," so long as they tithed and obeyed the Almighty's Word, which was the words from your lips, and so long as the women and their children obeyed the words of their priest, which was the word of men.

And you preached an end to liquor and tobacco, and you preached an end to "games of chance," and you preached an end to visits to "dens of iniquity," and you preached an end to novels, ladies' magazines, and all other "materials lewd and idea giving." Now you heard the grumbling of many, born of late nights at the brothers' house, the brothers themselves intoxicated on banned liquor proposing, "Perhaps what we need is a new Preacher." And when one man professed his belief that your word came from the lips of God a brother said, "Maybe what we need is a new god then."

So now you called the brothers before you. They were tall and loutish and cocky and swaggering, but you were the Revelator, and your book was the light of revelation, and into your heart reached that black creature, and now in tone cold and true you said, "Allow me to fill your days with a more splendid duty than loafing." And you told them you had considered at length this matter of "discipline," consulting His creature, who suggested you put together a trusted crew. So you told the brothers they were to head this crew, enforcing your laws and dictates with a "loving cruelty." And the louder of the brothers said, "Finally." Soon they went from house to house in black masks, kicking open doors, brandishing knives, piling wheelbarrows and wagons with what forbidden wares they did not confiscate into sacks and under coats. They built incineration piles in the center of the neighborhood, and while the whole of your neighborhood gathered you doused them with liquor and lit the flame, admonishing the wicked hearts of even your sturdiest followers.

And you preached against all other preachers and prophets and teachings. And you preached against those who worshipped the trees as gods. And you preached against those who shook and foamed and refused His commandment to multiply. And you preached against those who preached in churches and in temples, and you preached against those who called for the liberation and elevation of women, and you preached against those who called for the freedom of the African slave. And you preached against those who preached in tents. And you preached against those who studied the Word of the Almighty in schools, those "advisors" and "experts" and "gatekeepers" who claimed for themselves authority over the remission of sins. Who claimed they could conjure His blood and flesh from common household goods. And from their heaping coffers they crafted idols and golden faucets and other such obscenities coveted only by their sinful class. And what a lather you inspired, the cries of "Blood, blood, blood!" when you preached against the preachers, and the books of the preachers, and all the other churches and philosophers of the land. And when you said the ministers of the Evil One walked this land in the guise of agents of God, there were cries of "Let's get 'em!" Now you calmed them with the waving of your arms, saying, "Let us not respond with our wrath. At least, not until we are better prepared."

LIII. And when the other preachers heard this news they said amongst themselves, "It might be time we burn down that church," and they added, "But let's make sure all of them are in it." And they made plans. And they readied torches. And now when you walked their gentile streets you knew the pressure of their eyes, the gust of their whispers, even if their doings on loose inspection appeared as normal gentile doings.

LIV. And many priests now rose to preach the language of the Almighty. And some preached from scraps of paper. And some preached from memory, their eyes searching the ceiling. And others preached spontaneously. And some preached with voices so soft the congregation cupped their ears, the brothers in the back row shouting, "Speak up!" And some preached with red faces, thumping the pulpit. And others preached with stutters. And others preached mumbling. And many preached how the Almighty desired for "young lads to obey their fathers." And there were those who preached to "suffer not the gentiles." And there were those who preached the glory of the kingdom to come, for they had dreamed the top of His black mountain and known the spoils, the heaped golden splendor, and they had known their dead, in the guise of marvelous birds, perched there and watching.

LV. When your wife's hymnal, printed and bound, arrived in crates, the congregation sang. How quiet and blushing was this woman as she received her congratulations. And that evening as she ran her fingers over the pages, as if the grains of the paper did impart some further knowledge, she began to speak of perhaps a second hymnal. Now you spoke loudly over her thoughts: "Yes, perhaps it is time I wrote another book—there are so many revelations to tell. An excellent thought, my wife," and you kissed her brow.

"Of course, my husband," she whispered.

LVI. And when an awful breath of flame streaked the night sky, lighting the streets as in the day and making invisible all the stars, you began to preach the word of the end of time. For in the final hour man will become wicked and greedy, and the governments will be dissolved, and the good will hide in the mountains, subsisting on honey, pheasants, root vegetables. And the skies will light with balls of fire, and the skies will fall before periods of darkness. And while in years past the destruction came by flood, where man survived atop some mountain, or within some boat, this will prove the final hour for all. There will be earthquakes and fires, and there will be plagues, and bodies will swell fat with blackness and cough blood as thick and putrid as oil. And whatever man has domesticated will turn against him and assault him. Now man will fall against the gnashing of his hounds and his horses and his mules and his oxen, coughing blood and broken teeth beneath the furious trample of their teeth and hooves. And the creature of the Almighty will sharpen its horrid sickle. And bodies will fill the streets. And ships will drift with the deadweight of entire crews. And mothers will forsake their children. And wives will denounce their husbands. And entire populations will be sought out and murdered as scapegoats. And men will lash themselves with iron-spiked whips, spreading the ground with their blood, crying out, "Mercy! Mercy!" and "Peace! Peace!" They will claim to heal the dying and they will claim to raise the dead, and they will tell stories of their meals eaten with the Almighty. And they will murder priests. And they will ravish the flesh of their congregation, making bloody love to their parishioners. And many dead men and beasts will cover the

ground, the air rife with their pestilence. And when the last of
the people can find no food they will eat the last of the tree bark
and the final strands of grass. And then the wicked will murder their brothers, and these they will feast upon. And mothers
will eat their children, and wives will eat their husbands. And
tornadoes will diminish towns to the dust, and hurricanes will
pull cities into the sea. And the sea will blacken, and mountains will explode in fire, and locusts will fill the skies, until
ears bleed from the force of their hum. And from the heavenly
darkness shall come yellow eyes and the most ancient of beasts
will unhinge its jaws, devouring the sun and the moon. Now
the world will fall into winter. Now long hours of sleep, for
even the Almighty will weary. And when the last cock crows
upon the scarred land His ancient eye shall blink open, and He
will stand in judgment over the good and the wicked. And the
world shall be cast into flame. And the world shall be dissolved.
And from the molten ash the mountains will rise anew, and the
fields return shimmering. And the righteous will be called from
the soil, and the sinners will be cast into flaming pits. From the
loam the good will rise, as they were in life, nude but for the
shroud of soil, reborn and cast anew in the Almighty's image.
And the end will be known as the resurrection of the saints, and
the trumpets of His creature will radiate across the heavens.

LVII. And the brothers rose to preach a return to the
"grand old days" of offerings. With great long-
ing they recalled the final bleating struggle, the hot splash of
blood, and the rank, delicious burning flesh. How the brothers' eyes glowed, and their throats filled with blood. That night
they stumbled the streets, drinking from substances banned.
Here they beckoned to a stray dog with meat scraps and kissing
noises, and they seized the animal by the scruff, and they slit
that body gone limp, and blood gushed to the street. And they
folded their hands into trumpets, calling out, cackling, "O God,
O God, save us O God."

And when some came to you with this news you could only say, vaguely, "Yes, I see."

LVIII. Now others rose against you, claiming revelation contrary to your preaching. And many of these said, "The voice of the Almighty came to me in a flash of light." And some preached from sheets of paper they insisted contained the dictated message of the Almighty. Many were against the concept of the Almighty having once been a man of flesh. And others wanted the names of their wives and daughters returned, although no man sought to diminish man's dominion over woman. And others preached against the ban on substances. And others preached against tithing. And others abhorred the houses they shared, or the houses you put them in, for the Almighty insisted their families belonged in bigger houses, or more rustic houses, or warmer houses. And all insisted the Almighty had come unbidden, as they shaved or walked to work, or during the lulls of the afternoon hour, as a voice much like any other, perhaps even in their own voice. For you had once preached that men in the grip of revelation must trust the conviction in their hearts and that the language of their mind was also the true language of the Almighty.

And while these men preached you flushed crimson and shifted in your seat, and the brothers cheered from the back of the church.

LIX. And the more you preached of the divinity of man, the more revelations your congregation received, and soon you could not preach for the preaching of all the revelators in your midst. And many of these men now claimed the Almighty desired no "Preacher" at the head of His church, for all men should share in the making of laws and rules and revelations. And at this pronouncement you swayed and gnashed and foamed, and you shouted that you knew a bursting light and the stink of brimstone. Now you were "thrown" from the pulpit and you lay quivering on the floor, lost in some grim unconscious state. When you awoke you said you had wandered the mountain, and there He had warned a time of many false revelators had come. "I have seen your faces," you seethed. "He has shown me your ways, and dare you again speak, or mutter, or wink, or gaze in knowing ways, then He will extinguish us all." And now one of the brothers cried out, "It is true! There glows yonder mountaintop," although no temple window opened to His black mountain. And several men now murmured it was the truth, while a young boy wept and several young girls screamed at what they called "an awful light."

LX. That night the brothers told you of the many "fine young ladies" they had known since moving to your town. How "pliable" the girls were in your congregation. The brothers' slithering eyes and wet lips, their darting tongues. And the brothers described many methods of copulation foreign to your understanding—indeed, many instruments and tools. And they said, "Have you never heard? Why, there are books." And the vocal brother said, "Do you know how many wives those old prophets had?" How you blushed when the sister entered, offering you tea and a cake. Abruptly you rose. "This is all for tonight, gentlemen," you said. "My old bones get awful weary at these late hours." How strange you felt under the moonlight. How you seemed another man in the open air, as if you were barely alive.

And upon your return home, you shut your eyes and dreamed her consuming dinner or brushing her hair or curled upon her bed, dreaming of you. And you imagined the substance of her voice as she said your name. And you imagined the nature of her hand upon your own. And how your pulse quickened and your throat constricted, until your wife said, "My darling, how far away you seem."

LXI. Now you watched the shadows move and breathe on the ceiling. Horns and hooves and wings of black. The pacing fury of a creature that exhaled brimstone, whispering of what must come next.

LXII. And soon you preached that the Almighty desired the natives within the "western lands" to know the truth of their birthright. "The Almighty longs for His time on earth. The Old Man desires again to leave His mountain." You chose the brothers as His emissaries into the wilderness and named the vocal of these brothers as commander of the expedition. When you informed the congregation the vocal brother cried out: "Our luggage is prepared. He spoke to us as well." And all cheered this revelation. All welcomed the coming of light into darkness, for all godly welcome the end of time.

LXIII. And soon general stores were emptied by boys and men with rolled-up sleeves, dripping sweat in the October chill, as they piled wagons with burlap sacks of oats, dried beans and apricots, tinned peaches and jellied pork, pouches of tobacco, wheels of cheese, and casks of water, wine, whisky, and bundles of shirts and linens, and sleeping bags, and tarpaulins, and stakes, and boxes of nails. How still and silent the oxen in their yokes. The horses snorting, their bulging eyes. These brothers milled and guffawed, leered at the ladies and whispered sordid schemes, spat rosettes in the dust. And when they called for their sister you said, "Well, nothing was said of her—" and the brothers smiled: "He probably saved that revelation for us, don't you think, Preacher?" Their quiet knowing laughter, her black dress and veil-obscured eyes. And when she opened her mouth, there the line of her teeth as in fantasies long ago, and the curve of her youthful neck rose from the fumes of time, and there the black mark, as in those dead years past. How you welled up, saying, "This damned sun," although the clouds rolled heavy and gray. Soon she and her brothers and their cronies went into the dust, into the mystery of the western lands, into worlds you had written about but none could promise existed.

LXIV. Now in the evening you regaled your wife with dreams and proclamations as in days of old. And now you saw her for all you had known together. And you embraced her, kissing her cheeks, while the years flowered before you, the children raised and the children dead. "Oh, my wife," you said, "we are young yet, although we have seen our Isaac... grown into a man and left us," and you gestured in the direction you believed he must live. "Shall not our love some new life into this world?"

And soon her belly mounded, and soon this wailing creature pulled forth into the world, red and slick. And soon this infant was bathed. And soon this infant was swaddled. And when the midwife asked the child's name your wife began to say, "Elizabeth," and you said, "Daughter. For that is what she is."

LXV. Now as word of your preaching spread along the land, so too did the story of how the testament came unto you. So your name and story appeared on the front pages of the gentile newspapers, and there the gentile experts and gentile natural scientists and gentile philosophers and gentile preachers and gentile schoolteachers and gentile professors denounced your explanations and words as "obvious fabrications." And in town squares they derided your religion as a "confidence game." And in the press they mocked your prose as "rudimentary" and "childish," and your followers as puppets and dupes, for who could believe God would call a mere butcher, without education or degree, to translate such a text?

And the gentile priests sermonized about the ancient laws you sought overturned, and they preached how you preached of their illegitimacy, their corruption, and their coming damnation, and the damnation of all who followed them, and the damnation of all who did not follow you. And they scoffed, "He does not believe in burnt offerings, yet he claims to know the ways of God?" Services along the land were interrupted by crazed, indignant cries, and some threw hymnals, and many stomped their boots, and others screamed, "Let's tie 'em up!"

And the gentiles called every man of your flock a scoundrel and a threat to their rule, for you kept to yourselves, and during elections your priests voted only for those men the Almighty told you to vote for, and your priests shopped only at shops owned by your priests. Yes, your way was the ruination of democracy, and your way led only to oppression. And you responded, "The Almighty never spoke of separating the church from the state."

And gentiles accused you of "corrupting" their young, for whenever you saw a gentile lad on the street you handed him your book, saying, "This is the best way to avoid hellfire, lad," and when this did not work, you said, "Say, I bet you like pretty girls, don't you?"

And now gentiles sent letters to the editors of newspapers decrying your influence, insisting you and your followers must be "driven from our valley." And the editors called your influence "shadowy." And they called your followers "warped" and "dangerous." And now gentiles lurked in the shadows, tossed bricks through windows with twine-fastened notes reading "leave hear" in charcoal lettering. And they set barrels ablaze, rolled these through your streets, embers cascading and smoke spiraling, while children and women watched the glow through parlor windows. And your priests gathered their muskets and rifles and bowie knives. And they bunkered behind porches. And they roamed the streets, shouting, "Show yourselves, gentile dogs!" And the gentiles uprooted your gardens, and the gentiles pulled the bungs from your casks of ale and cider, and the gentiles left your pet dogs buzzing with flies. And they menaced your followers on public roads by whispering phrases like

"I would watch myself" and "Heard the weather's mighty nice out west" in passing.

And you waited for the creature and no more did the rough wings beat. And you called for the brothers and heard only silence. And you called for Harris and he was moldering. And when you stood before your wife, she said, "These gentiles mean to impoverish us. They want to take our house, and diminish the inheritance of our son." Against you now she pressed, "You are our shepherd. Now, darling, a shepherd deals roughly with wolves."

So you gathered the cruelest and the stealthiest of your priests, and when gentile bodies were found sprawled on the streets and rotting in fields, headless and emptied of blood, none could cease whispering of your "avenging angels."

And fights between your priests and the gentiles broke out in the streets and shops, men rolling in the mud, on floorboards, your priests beaten with pipes and planks of wood, your priests left moaning, spitting black blood, eyes mashed in and lips split, burst and gushing. Stray dogs slunk through the streets, wagging tails and licking wounds. And gentile children scampered about, giggling and thrashing bleeding priests with hickory. And these priests moaned and waved at the children, and the children spat in return, calling the priests "devils."

Now you barricaded yourself within your home. When supplies were needed you sent your wife, and you delivered all new revelations via envelope, with your crest, the lion, pressed into red wax. And when commanded by the Almighty you positioned four husky priests before the entrance of your home. These priests hefted pistols and pipes, their expressions a mystery beneath the slouch hat shadows. And you told them to "shoot on sight" any gentile who wandered near. How many shots were fired, the shells gathered into mounds, the gun smoke a choking fog. And there were those who said to clear the world of gentiles would mean to clear the world of people, for the doctors were gentiles, and the professors, and the mayors, and the senators, and the architects, and the schoolteachers, and the newspaper editors. And indeed all those who wrote laws and passed laws and enforced laws were gentiles, and these gentiles now decreed the eradication of you and your church. And you offered this decree to the greater nation as proof of your persecution. Now stampeding hooves and rifle fire, now taut ropes and sharpened knives. Soon none could find the mayor, or his family, and his house was burned to ash while his faithful hound roamed the streets, half blazed to blistered flesh, wagging its hairless tail and whimpering for alms.

And the police raided your possessions, and the police smashed your icons, and they battered your priests, led them to jail bleeding from busted lips. And jeering crowds spat. Nights now in feces-and-blood-smeared cells, listening to flies, skittering rats. And the police fired pistols into your neighborhoods, their faces covered by hoods or smeared with black polish, glinting in the firelight like pooled oil, whooping in alien tongues they believed mimicked native languages.

And when the names and addresses of policemen became known, now too their bodies were found in fields, fly covered and headless.

Now your priests found their shops and places of employ set ablaze, and now into ruin and ash while the fire department stood by with water wagons and horse-drawn engines, smoking cigars and telling jokes, ignoring those priests pleading for help. And when the flames rose to impressive heights firefighters wet the neighboring rooftops of gentile-owned buildings. And policemen pulled your priests from the blaze, beat them with billy clubs, and tossed them into the paddy wagon, gasping and sooty and drooling blood.

And policemen brandished their billy clubs and stroked the edges of their pistols from your steps, and they called into bullhorns that if you ever preached from your book they would arrest you, and none could be certain of your fate, for "many mishaps happen in jails." And while your wife held you back you opened your shirt and laid bare your breast. And you said, "Draw your pistols upon me if you will." And you said, "Kill me, I am not afraid to die, and I have endured so much oppression that I am weary of life. But I am more lion than man, and from the mountain of my fathers I will cast you down." So these officers merely repeated their warnings and left without further harm. Once indoors you stared into the shadows, and you did not weep or shake, but from your mouth now such a horrid, lonesome sigh that your wife called from the kitchen, "What has happened?"

Now you summoned your priests around. "The Almighty desires some quiet on our part," you said. "He does not wish to see His Revelator come to harm." And there was a great uproar. These men with blotched eyes and torn apart lips, bloody bandaged arms and legs and brows, suggested you "reconsult," for "we have already shed much blood" and they "heard no weeping from His mountain." So your parlor was filled with such men, looking upon you harshly.

And when you next stood before them at the pulpit you thumped your book and railed against the gentiles and their wickedness. You said the gentiles would be cast into fires and brimstone, for the Almighty was no small plant to be bent by "malicious winds." And you said, "Our will, our conviction, our mission cannot be detoured by the acts of the damned." And you said, "The time for conversion is done. We stand at opposite ends and there they lie for us in the weeds. Lo, behold their great wickedness—" and you gestured to the rows of bloodied and battered priests, and women who lost their homes, and children who slept not for the nightmares of masked riders in the night, the pistol shots of policemen, and their fathers, arrested and flogged and hanged. And your temple quaked with applause and hooting, and men shouted: "You tell 'em, Preacher," and "Give 'em what for!" The shadows of the gentile police loomed as you said, "I come to you waving not an olive branch, but brandishing the sword of His everlasting vengeance." And then the shadows disappeared.

LXVI. They came for you as you slept, beating open your door with logs. And they spilled into your parlor, grunting, shouting, and they smashed in your windows, while their torches licked and scorched and painted the ceilings black. And they shouted your name and not the name your followers called you. And some came hooded. And some came black polish painted. And of those who came undisguised you recognized many as followers who disputed the suppression of spirits and tobacco. And they pulled your wife struggling and screaming from her bed. And they pulled Daughter from bed, her skull striking the floor. And now a man hefted the limp child. And you shouted, "Oh my Father, protect me!" as they grabbed your arms, as they slapped you across the face, as they punched you in the belly. They dragged your wife outdoors and cast her into the street, weeping for Daughter. And Daughter struck the cobbles with a dull, loose thump, bouncing once. And she did not thrash. And she did not wail. And you cried out through your tears, "Oh please don't kill me!" They brought you now into the streets, dragged you past your wife, your daughter, pulled you through the jeering throngs that kicked you in the ribs, in the face, that stomped your back, until you could no longer scream. And after they stripped you naked they brought forth a copper pot bubbling with hot pine tar. This they poured over your body entire, coating your chest, your back, your genitals, and down your legs and feet. And the seething. And the fumes. And they spat upon you, saying, "You should have listened to us." Now they said your name and not the name your followers called you. And they pried your mouth open with their hands. And you bit them until they stopped. And they jabbed a funnel into your face, your lips bloodied and mashed, your mouth yet clamped. Finally they cast the funnel aside and poured the pitch over your head, and they slit open pillows, and now the feathers gathered about your figure. And they promised the next time you preached they would "put a rifle in your mouth." And they said, "We'll spatter the streets with you." So they left you, writhing and smoldering and nude, and so your followers found you, stinking of burned skin and pine tar. And your wife screamed for she thought you coated in dried blood. Your followers attended to her, feverish and fainted in bed, while you peeled free the tar and feathers, the floor soon covered with the black and blistered shell of your flesh.

LXVII. You did not ask after Daughter, and if you had they would have said, "She is sleeping." for indeed she lay silent and still, although by the morning that followed she had not waked and she would never again. And while your wife wept and prayed you went to the yard. And there you sat until the eyes of wives and widows pressed upon you, and then you moved on. And you walked the forests, your flesh moaning in the open air, and there you understood His language in the wind, the scurrying of animals, the musk of leaves and dirt. And when you did not immediately return many believed you would resign as Preacher. And many believed you would quit the valley altogether, as so many false prophets and revelators had done before. And many believed you would return for your wife and son. And many believed you would not.

Yes, now you walked until you came to a clearing. Your brow pressed to the ground. "O Father," you said. "O God." And here there waited no creature. And here no voice vibrated from the mountain. Here only silence and the crawling of things.

LXVIII. And when you returned your wife could say only, "She is unmoving." Now you, scorched and yet tar stinking, carried the blanket-bound remains of Daughter into the yard. Into the soil without ceremony, beyond the digging of a hole and the uttering of the words of your book: "You were raised from the ashes of this world and you are returned the ashes of this world." And you held your wife, who did not speak, your arm about her waist. Oh, that familiar warmth. "We shall see her again, Wife," you said. "She is with Him now." And you gestured to the mountain, the cruel lines of that peak.

"But will we know her," your wife wept, "full grown and by then ladylike?"

"Her soul shall know us, Mother," you said. "And we will know hers."

LXIX. In the hours to follow, all awaited your arrival, seated silent in the shadows of your temple. And many men who had thrashed you and rolled you in tar and feathers sat in attendance, waiting to take possession of your church when you did not arrive. And little was said, and there was much coughing and shifting of bodies and anxious breathing. And then you arrived, scorched and blistered, leaning upon your wife in mourning costume. And all stood. And some gasped. And many former assailants from the night prior began to edge out of their seats. And some women wept at your scars while priests gaped in astonishment. At the pulpit, your eyes glistened while in a ravaged voice you spoke: "You don't know me; you never knew my heart. No man knows my history. I cannot tell it; I shall never undertake it. I don't blame anyone for not believing my history. If I had not experienced what I have, I could not have believed it myself." And your voice shook, and your fist thumped the pulpit, and you announced, "When I am called by the trump of the creature and weighed in the balance, you will all know me then."

BOOK III
THE GENERAL

I. So in those days your motto became that of the old prophets: "When they persecute you in one city gather what you
must and flee to the next." And so went the years: issuing the
call to depart, church bells clanging, even as your shops and
houses were torched by gentile mobs. And the children wept.
And the oxen trudged. And your priests cursed the gentiles. And
the women remained silent.

And when you had fled the last of the cities beneath the black
mountain you described a place beyond the known expanse, and
ordered a flight into the depth of the unknown. And when your
priests brought you maps you said, "This land resides beyond all
maps." And when they said, "How will we possibly find it?" you
answered, "He will guide our way."

And so this final time you gathered into wagons, the slow
trudge and silent resignation. And when rations lowered your
priests rode into the prairies with their rifles. And when a deer
or rabbit or grouse strayed along the range, soon the spasm and
plummet of the animal: bloody mouth opening and closing, the
ebbing light of its eyes, your feasts on the fire-scorched remains,
from which your son alone abstained. He alone became gaunt,
subsisting on boiled weeds. And to your son, stooped over his
gurgling pot, you whispered, "Who are you? From whose flesh
do you actually originate?"

And the farther west you trudged the less familiar were the
animals, and here the deer were bizarrely striped and here their
heads were fashioned with horns spiraling and horns long and

curling. And here packs of dogs scampered, or what your men called "near-dogs," lingering on the hillsides, their arched backs and red gums. Here a land vast and strange, untamed by man and as if forgotten by God. And on the wind of the night came the snarling noise of dogs eviscerating some weaker beast, and how the children wept for this new and constant horror. These children you comforted, saying, "Be calm, for there is no beast of grander terror than that creature who guides our way."

11. And those who had stood by you from the start became sentimental, remembering during these nights on the open range those early months, camped on your lawn while you composed your book. And now to them you preached, "In the darkness of our trials, never forget how He brought you to me, how He bade you linger, how He gave you strength against your hours of doubt." And you said, "And this is what I remember in those hours when I am weighed down by our task, our suffering, our sorrows: I remember gazing at the tents of perhaps a hundred men I did not know. Men who desired only to share in the word and blessing of the life and world to come." And you said, "And I knew then we would see our promises fulfilled."

Now you passed the tracks of forgotten peoples: wandering tribes, the ancient men who prefigured your nation, those men cast from the original lands and grown into the people you called the natives. "The tracks of our fathers and mothers," you said. And you called mounds of dirt and dead grass "the graves of great priests," while elsewhere you gestured to rock formations smeared with black and red images, and you pointed to these pictographs, saying, "Had I my glasses I could translate these." While elsewhere you saw the remnants of what you called an illustration of first fathers, wearing armor and plumes. And you continued past enormous rocks strewn along the barren land, "the last remnants of a great city." And you said, "No human eye has looked upon these ruins in a thousand years."

And when the wild dogs neared your camp you saw they were similar to foxes but speckled and stripped, their hair tufted and wild. They stalked the edges of the horizon, and some nights you believed they pawed at your tent, so you sent your wife to inspect. She found only the rustling of wind and weeds and dust. And in the night the firing of shots, the yelping of strange animals, and in the morning your priests found only blood trails and tufts of fur.

Deeper now into the western lands, and no further revelation came. Into the west, now, into the land of skulls and bones, the remnants of enormous animals, and the distant stampedes of these same beasts shook your tents apart. When later your priests found these vast woolly bison grazing, they shot them and shot them again until finally the creatures lay dying with distended tongues and wide milky eyes; soon the guts strewn and the skin rotting and the meat smoked over fires.

Deeper west, you found only bones.

And then the cracked-open landscapes, the dry weeds and creeping insects, the enormous birds, long necks and red misshapen heads, circling silently overhead.

And when you found the skull and rib bones of a vast and mysterious creature they seemed the bones of some monster predating all but the first father and mother of man. You knelt before ribs and tusks and skull, each greater than any man, and finally you called out: "Our Father's imagination is without equal!"

III. And when your stores of meats—smoked and salted—went, now only mealy flour remained. Now prairie flowers and thistles were boiled and consumed, and then the earth upturned and the worms of the soil eaten where they wriggled. And then the water casks were dry.

Still you continued into these landscapes, devastated and scarred, where no man or animal could survive.

And half-starved children chased loose woods and rolled empty water casks along the jagged earth, while men sat before their fires and openly wondered if they had been misled. And some wondered if the Almighty had ceased speaking to you, and others murmured perhaps you were a fraud after all. Now you summoned your avenging angels and soon the mouth of discontent quieted.

And then the shadow of the creature returned, and now again, the dread light of its eyes.

IV. Now a rider was sighted, blurred and distant along the bleached rocks. Women and children were sent into the tents while the priests armed themselves. And all agreed you possessed a "tremendous calm" as you said, "I will meet him." So you rode to this fellow, his slouch hat and whiskered face. He handed you a weathered note proclaiming that the brothers had become as kings here in the western lands, preaching the truth of your word in the back of the general store they owned. "For some days now we have known of your approach," read the note. "It will be good to see you again, brother."

V. And while the brothers and their followers prepared welcoming banners and songs on fife and drum, the gentiles of this town readied their pistols. And the gentiles commented on your frenzied eyes, your wild shocks of hair, while from atop a crate you announced, "Be easy, brothers, for a new light is at hand." And your hands flailed and spittle flew, and you gestured to the scattered houses and shops and saw mills and the dirt streets strewn with manure and mud, and you said, "See here, this land, our birthright. See here our land of milk and honey." And you directed your priests to draw up plans for "a dozen, dozen more houses." And you directed your priests to prepare for the "erection of a new temple."

Now the gentiles smiled. "By whose right do you intend to do all this?" they asked. And you gestured to the black mountain in your old grand way, saying, "By His." But the gentiles' brows merely furrowed, and they looked around as if lost, claiming no knowledge of any such mountain or god as of you now spoke. Yet you saw it, and the brothers saw it, and all their followers saw it, and all of your pilgrims, weary and half-dead as they were, saw it. So to the gentiles, ignorant and forsaken, you laughed. "You see?" you called out. "We have been chosen, and you have been damned."

VI. And it was said these western gentiles too did not burn offerings, but not out of commandment of God, but out of preciousness of livestock.

VII. And as your population swelled your people raised new houses and prepared the temple. Soon most of the shops of the town belonged to you, and the houses were yours in majority, and soon your priests wrote in journals: "The gentiles watch our growing prosperity and power with greed and an avaricious eye." And as your coffers swelled so did the number of temples you commanded built, from one to five to twelve. While of the gentiles you said, "We have dealt with them before," although your people had always lost these conflicts.

And you became gray and lined. You developed sags, a paunch. And the creature wandered with you always, whispering in your ear, lingering in the shadows, and dripping oil from your ceiling.

And you ruled as a king in this last city. Here you decreed no liquor, or gambling, or brothels, and if some devil opened a brothel you burned it down. And the ladies of these houses, in their lace and rouge, their eyelids heavy with blue, you established in the spare rooms of the houses of your priests, whom you bade watch over and protect these "wretched, unfortunate women," and teach them "the skills and the handicrafts required of a daughter, or mother, or sister, or wife, in the eyes of the Almighty."

And the girl you took in was said to be no more than sixteen, blond and blue eyed and rosy lipped. And when she trembled at your feet you told her some joke until she smiled upon you. Now you took her by the hand, saying, "You will come with us, my child."

And while your wife spoke that night you listened to her not, so thick was the blood in your ears, your throat. You watched only the lines of her face, the gray hairs.

And there were those who said you went to this girl while your wife slept, and there you lay with her as a man does with a woman, and there were those who claimed you whispered the language of your endearment to her, traced the lines of her palms and cupped the swell of her breasts. Others said you dressed this girl in a white gown, and there married her by commandment of the Almighty. And there were those who said you confessed to them, "Some time ago He commanded me to commit myself to the sacred practice of plural marriage." And there were those who said you claimed you could not bring yourself to carry out this commandment until you saw this girl before you, lost and lonesome, until you felt what you called "love" flowering within. And you knew then the wisdom of His commandments, the promise of your lives through eternity.

But when the women of your church accused you as an adulterer you denied the charge as "unfounded" and "perverse." And there were those who called this "a dirty, nasty, filthy affair." And there were those who claimed they would no longer build your temple, or work within the stores or mills or banks, or at any other task you commanded, until you sent this blond girl away.

And your first wife said, "If this is true I will sever your member while you sleep." And you patted her knee: "How my sweet dove chirrups! Of course there is no truth to it!" And so you arranged for this girl to join a family in another settlement. And you patted the girl's hand, and your wife embraced her as sisters embrace, while the girl cried out, "Oh, Papa, don't send me away." Coolly you saw her into the carriage. "You see," you told your wife, "she meant nothing to me." That night your priests pleaded of you, "My Prophet, don't send our girls away too!"

And there are those who said you confessed the truth had been revealed and registered in your book, but "I fear others must step forward first before the Great Revelation gains traction." And you said, "My brothers, we must be strong against the winds of prejudice and fear." And only then could they keep their girls, and further obtain what other ladies they had dreamed of having.

And many priests dreamed a "magnificent revelation," telling their wives the Almighty had said through a "man alone may a woman obtain entrance to the black mountain." And now out of the charity of their hearts many priests took second wives. And some took thirds. And some took the sisters of old wives, or cousins, or aunts, and one took a mother, and some took widows, and some took orphaned barn girls, or milkmaids, or stray prostitutes, or even gentile ladies long coveted by your men. And some traded their own newly flowering sisters for the barely budded daughters of other priests. No priest dared condemn you, although some held on to their lone wife and called this revelation "a travesty," whispering amongst themselves of a "darkness rising" in their midst.

And some claimed they heard the creature's hooves on their rooftops, while the flames of judgment rained down from its yawning breath.

VIII. Through the turmoil they continued building your temple. And while the men constructed, the women labored in their way: knitting, spinning, sewing, and preparing and carrying food on platters to the men. You watched the progress from a window a half-mile distant, copper spyglass unfurled, and when concluded you stood before your new temple, your final temple, and you cried out, "My brethren, the spirit of the Almighty is burning." And to the black mountain you said, "And let Thy house be filled with a rushing mighty wind with Thy glory." And the congregation shouted, "Hosanna to the Almighty!"

IX. And in those years all of faith and devotion prospered. And all grew fat. And in your presence the creature too became corpulent, belly rotund and glistening. It crouched and glowered in the corner of every room you attended, ever expanding, but never eating. And you lived now in the whitest house atop the hill. And your priests likewise lived in mansions, and they prospered in their shops and investments, in their marriages.

And when you saw a gentile on the street you would stop him and gesture to your mansion. "You see where I live?" you would say. And to the newspapers and politicians and university professors who mocked and derided your work you sent illustrations of your home, the gold dinnerware you ate off, the monies within your coffers, the live lions caged and circling in your "den." And you said unto these gentiles, "You see now what I have become. You see how the Almighty favors me and how He despises you."

And you had a library filled only with books of your composition. This room you attended often, running your fingers along the spines, the gold lettering of your name, and to yourself you whispered of your days within the barn, nurturing in the hay and gloom a greatness known only to you.

Now the gentiles "lamented" your prosperity, and their slick, pompous politicians sought to limit your powers, or control your authority, or tax you into submission. You commanded the coffers emptied, announcing, "I will not be persecuted any longer!" And now you emptied your coffers, ordering uniforms and rifles and swords. And you sent commissioned portraits of you and your assembled army to the gentile capital with a note suggesting none should dare intrude upon your sovereignty.

And the gentile president held this portrait for long minutes before he sighed, saying, "We may have to do something about this fellow."

And no man dared confront you. And the women eyed your heft, your wise lines and gray hair, glorious.

Now you walked the streets with a bulldog trotting at your side. So you called this beast a "gentile eater," gloating it would "rend flesh from the bone of any gentile man, woman, or child." And you set it upon a gentile lad who snickered at your girth. So you exalted at his screams, the thrashing and hot spurt of his blood. And now you paraded, at home and in the streets, in full uniform, with ostrich plume and shining sword, with muskets readied. And your congregation cheered and whistled and cried out, "Show 'em what for, Prophet!" And your soldiers boasted they would fire with "great malice" upon any who molested them. And your soldiers cried, "Beware, oh earth! How you fight against the saints of the Almighty and shed innocent blood." And the gentile faces drained white.

Now you took daily audience with your angels, who reported on gentile doings—the mayor, the sheriff, the shopkeepers, the blacksmith, and all those who held power, and all those who held a prejudice against your kind.

Ever now you took counsel from the creature—its rasped utterings and clacking hooves, the stink of brimstone issuing from your office. And now your office nearly filled with its obsidian bloat, so your desk had to be removed from the room, and you stood pressed against the wall. Ever now its red eyes flared as the creature whispered how you should blot from the earth all gentiles, and you should march on their capital, raze it to the ground, and you should run for president of the entire nation, stand as king so the Almighty could flower within the hearts of all. Ever now that yammering, ever now that droning sound, that sick noise, that voice in the pulse of blood, that language of all the terrible longings of the heart.

X. As you increased in power and ambition, so your family increased in number. Now you populated your home with women your wife referred to as "ladies in need." And no matter how many you added you always knew their names for, no matter the girl, her name was always "Wife." Your first wife called these ladies her "hundred sisters," and they called her "our aged mother." And these wives took turns bathing you and clothing you and feeding you and bedding you, while you boasted to your soldiers that your wives "gladly" coupled with you, and all at once, and in all positions, and through all hours, if you desired, but you were no longer young, and such delights would likely kill you.

And you told one girl, "I know what it means to be orphaned, but one hundred women will have to die before I am a widower."

And the rooms of your mansion brimmed with wives, and some called you "Preacher," and some called you "Husband," and the youngest and newest of these called you "General" and with these you wore your plumes to bed. And it was said some days your first wife accepted these girls, and it was said some days she demanded they leave and she threw their clothing from the windows. And there were days she wept on the back porch. And there were days she yelled, "I will burn this house and all of your whores with it," so you sent her revelations from the Almighty condemning her "childish outbursts" and demanded she remember her "place" as your "helpmeet."

And to her final hour your first wife denied you took on wives so numerous, for you were never such a man as to "wound" her so terribly, and she was never such a woman as to allow such a "besmirching" of your love to occur.

And there were times when another wife woke covered in tar, or with her sheets on fire, or confronted by a coyote loosed in her chambers, or bald for in the night she was sheared clean. And some girls wept openly to you for the old wife's "coldness" and "jealousy," for you visited her chambers now only when your reading glasses were there or one of your nice shirts hung in the closet.

XI. And when the brothers married their sister to an aged farmer for the dowry of a hundred head of cattle, she went to the river, her pockets weighted with stones, her fingers slick with muck. She was seen in the moonlight by some onshore and then she was not seen. And soon her body found tangled in debris and pale and yet breathing. And you went to her side, and she was pale and shivering and otherwise much as she had ever been. And you began to say the name she had been born with before you realized this you had never known. And now you sent a dowry of four flour sacks filled with gold coins to her brothers and husband, claiming her as your own. And that first night she went to bed still outfitted in her widow's dress, the collar tight to the top of her throat. And she said, "I did not ask for this. I asked for none of this." And you replied, "You wear a black mark upon your throat, yes?" and when she nodded you said, "Well, let me see it." And so she did.

XII. And the gentile population too swelled, and now rival papers railed against your "black heart," your "wives" and "empirical ambitions," and suggested you should be "put down." So you had their gentile offices razed to the earth.

XIII. And on the day of the nation's birth, as your people and gentiles alike gathered for children's choirs and fife and drum music, now the brothers rose to the bandstand, brandishing their swords and passing a bottle of whisky between them. So now their fury was unbridled and they cried out, "My brothers, can you stand by and suffer such infernal devils! To rob men of their lives and rights. We have no more time for comment. Every man will make his own. Citizens, arise one and all: let it be made with powder and ball! Between us and them a war of extermination until the last of their blood is spilled or they will have to exterminate us. Our cheeks have been given to the smiters and our heads to those who have plucked off our hat. We have not only, when smitten on one cheek, turned the other, but we have done it again and again until we are wearied of being trampled on. But from this day and hour we will suffer it no more. And that mob that comes on us to disturb us shall be driven from the earth." And now the brothers bellowed with wordless fury and thrust their swords to the heavens, while you leapt to your feet, clapping and crying out "Hosanna!" And the others of your church roared likewise, while the gentiles watched in silent horror.

XIV. To the priests who married most frequently you gave plush positions within your administration. And those who supported the eradication of the gentile dogs you called "brother," promising them much "glory" in the life to come. And you told these men, "Your days upon the mountain will be spent in the company of your most comely wives, and you will live on mounds of jewels, and sleep on beds of gold, and all your pleasures and fantasies will be seen to." And when the less avowed of these men asked, "What of the other wives?"—for some did love rather than resent, or despise, or avoid the aged, or the portly, or the homely flesh they had wed.—to these men you said, "I suppose they can be there also, if you wish."

And gentile politicians and newspapers denounced your people, and the gentiles spat upon your priests and ransacked their stores, and ravaged their wagons and carriages, and stole their horses, and kissed and fondled and beat their wives, leaving the women bleeding in the streets.

And soon men on either side carried always knives and muskets and clubs. And now gentile mobs terrorized your homes with torches, burned your barns and fields. And militias surrounded your outer settlements, and when your people fled in wagon trains the soldiers fired upon them with muskets and hacked them with knives and burned their goods. They slaughtered the women and children, even the infants, and left them strewn without burial. Now carrion birds and wild dogs gorged on priests and wives and babes, while gentiles smoked cigars and laughed at the scene.

When the messenger came with the news of the slaughter he found you in your office, seated upon the creature's lap, nude but for the soot you smoldered in and the black tar that dripped from the creature's lips. And over your head the creature's tongue did wag, and through your hair its breath did gust. "We will kill them all," you said from within the creature's fat obsidian folds.

XV. Now none could escape your angels' fury, and many a gentile farm was burned to the ground, and many wives raped and beheaded, and their children beaten and beheaded, and the men themselves shot and beheaded. And their fields were burned. And their animals were slaughtered. These conquered beasts you served as the main courses at your victory banquets. Attired in full uniform, you drank much wine at these occasions, and toasted all your priests and all their dead, and all their wives and all of yours, and you waved your custom-built pistols, their high polish shining in the chandelier light. Now as the evenings waned you went from priest to priest, hugging them, telling them of your devotion. And after the last of these dinners you packed your clothing and a copy of your book into a trunk, and you called for the youngest of your wives to "ready the carriage."

And when the militias had not yet marched upon your house, nor ravaged your possessions, nor taken hold of your wives, you fled on horseback with three of your priests, leaving the brothers and your son to watch over your flock. And now you and your priests camped on hillsides, eating beans cooked in tins and drinking water from flasks, cool and metallic. And you rode still farther. And there were those who said you rode to the gentile capital, and there were those who said you sought the governor, and still others said you were "fleeing to the coast," where you intended to change your name and live out the rest of your days, anonymous and at peace, for you had forgotten the creature could track you from the mist of clouds.

And you could not know how your wives panicked, how they gathered in rooms, weeping and crying and holding one another, some as sisters in mourning, and some as something much more. And none allowed that they had been deserted. And none dared observe how the Almighty was silent in this hour.

XVI. And while you and your men camped a rider approached, waving a white flag. Still you commanded, "Shoot," and soon he sprawled coughing blood. To his chest he clutched a letter from your first wife, condemning your "cowardice," for "a shepherd's place is by his flock." And she insisted you return, otherwise "we will lose our way," and "if you do not return and submit to the law we will surely be slaughtered."

Now of the fellow nearest you asked, "What shall we do?"

"We must return and give ourselves up," he answered in his simplicity.

"But we will be butchered!"

And the man pressed your hand between his, and in a tone calm he said, "Surely the Almighty will watch over us."

XVII. And you prayed. And you called out, "He says nothing." And you wept. And you felt ill. Now you lay in the shade of the elms, yellow and green grasses trembling, squirrels skittering, black lines of ducks in flight, their glorious long-off song. And now when you inhaled you knew the very air was alive and the entire world writhed beneath you. "Such is His name," you said with a sigh to the men before you, "writ in the organism of His every invention." And now your greater sigh, for it came as one condemned: "Aye, there is no escaping such as Him."

So you returned and submitted to the governor's will. And several small cannons and hundreds of rifles were given over by your people, but you told your followers to hide their pistols in the straw of their mattresses, or fixed within their chimneys. You told them, "The blood of vengeance will yet tar the earth," and you promised the days of the gentiles "number in the few."

And so you and your three men were manacled and led

through the streets. There you were heckled and spat upon, and in the turmoil you said loudly so all could hear, "O Father, where are Thee?" And the sheriff and five guards locked you four into a horse-drawn wagon, and you traveled two days into the unknown. In the evenings you were fed beans and bacon, and you told stories and joked with your captors although they would not answer questions about your fate. They sat up until the sky swelled pink, drinking whisky from a bottle they passed to you and your priests, and when one of your priests said, "The Almighty has forbidden—" your captors replied, "It'll go easier this way." Now you took the bottle, and how it burned and how you longed for more, even as your captors handed it to your men. Now the faithful followed your example. When you finished drinking, when you could not feel your face or your hands, your captors bade you close your eyes and set your brow against a rock. And when you hesitated they forced your brow to the moss. And now came the click of the pistol, and the muzzle, cool and heavy against your brow. So you did not murmur His name, nor did you confess the nature of your transgressions, but you repeated your first wife's name in eternal cadence. And it was the name she was born with, the name you called her in the long-ago hours when you were scarcely yet a man. And when you thought you would perish from the earth the men simply laughed and fired their pistols into the air. How the terror seized you, made you small, and laughing still the captors mocked your stink, told you to "clean yourself up." They led you to the wagon, carrying you for the weakness in your knees. And now the long silence of your journey, when none spoke, and none dared look into the others' eyes.

XVIII. You and your fellows were brought to the debtor's room of the jailhouse. Outside the gentiles gathered in mobs—their torchlights and taunts and cries. And some burned you in effigy, while others called out, "String him up!" And the crowd whooped and laughed and fired pistols into the air. And you pleaded with the sheriff to move you to safer quarters or to "increase our protection at least," and the sheriff responded by sending away all but three of your guards. These remaining guards smiled and winked through the bars. And to the priests in your cell you asked, "Are you afraid to die?" and these men began to answer no until you said, "Do not lie in your final hour. The Almighty has raised us up to treasure life and there is no need to pretend otherwise." Now these men admitted they feared death, and one said, "I feel like I'm going to get sick," and another began weeping and you said, "I would weep too if I could," and you said, "But fear wraps me too tightly," and you said, "Brothers, I can scarcely breathe," and you said, "O my brothers, I can scarcely speak these words," and you said, "O brothers, I fear in death we become no more than a house to flies."

XIX. And the guards would not bring you paper or pen, but they took dictation. And now you said, "This is to my wife," and the guards laughed: "Which one?" And you winced. And you said, "To my first wife." And you said the name she was born with. And you said, "My heart has ever been yours." And you said, "These others, there were no others, beside me, through all our days," and you said, "We have loved and birthed and suffered and buried much—" and you said, "I will miss you with all my heart through the hours of my waiting," and you said, "But I shall know you again, in the world to come." And this letter was sealed and the guards promised it was carried forth by a trusted messenger.

But your first wife later claimed she never received such a note.

XX. And one night you drifted to sleep, and when you woke you saw the creature, fat and brimstone stinking before you. It drooled tar, and now it seemed to pull your comrades apart, consumed them entire, heads and legs, torsos and bellies, drank the blood and slurped the guts. And when they were gone the insatiable beast alone remained. "Come," the creature beckoned. "For I hunger again."

Now again you awoke, and for such long minutes they could not stop your screaming.

XXI. And another night you dreamed your cell unlocked and the misty fingers of dawn drew you outdoors. So you walked the long roads and the forests, a hundred miles you walked, and you did not weary nor did your feet bleed. Finally you stood at the mountain's base, and now you climbed three days and three nights. And at the peak there was neither light nor creature nor voice nor branches readied for an offering. There came only the winds, and the mists, and the screams of the carrion birds circling below.

XXII. Then the mob came for you with black-painted faces, guns, and torches, and they called your name in the sounds of jackals: *"Jooooooooo-sssssssseeeeeeeeeeeppppppphhhhh."* And they slaughtered the men on guard. And they shot one of your priests and the others yelled for you to flee for safety. So you climbed into the window as they filled you with bullets. And you fell to the court-yard, shot to pulp, and your blood thickened in the dust. Now gentiles circled, screaming and cheering and hooting, their faces smoldering in the torchlights. When the militia colonel arrived he ordered his men to lift you against the wall. There you stood, broken necked, lifeless, your eyes fat black with dirt, your mouth slumped open. And they fired upon you to "remove any doubt," not ceasing until you collapsed in a heap of blood.

And they buried you in the yard just deep enough for the dogs to scent you, the blond soil mounded and fresh and beckoning to the grave robbers.

You were thirty-eight when you died.

BOOK IV
THE BOOK
OF SAMUEL

I. In the hours following your death the sun bloomed red and later the rising moon seemed composed of blood. And when no priests would attend to your remains your first wife went alone, fending off dogs and gentile children with a shovel. And she did not weep when she brushed the soil from your bruised and bloody face, nor when she cleansed your body entire, nor when she knew how cold and unresponsive your skin, nor when she understood what crawled within, nor when she wrapped you in blankets, nor when she, grunting and sweating and panting, pulled you onto the sled and bound you with rope. Only as she fled did she weep. And only before you in your pine box did she beat her breast, rent her clothing and hair, and cried to no one in particular of what had become of the world she had known.

You were placed in the earth and covered over. A simple marker was erected, and upon this was written the name and birth date you had given yourself and the death date bestowed by fate and gentiles alike. Beneath the red sun, the vocal brother sermonized that these were glad times, and now he gestured to the black mountain only your followers could see, and he said, "Our beloved Preacher is with Him now."

And now the sun returned to its former hue. Only then did the men and women of the congregation believe you were truly saved.

II. In the days to follow most priests claimed visions or dreams inspired, ordaining them "Leader" and "Preacher," and your son was amongst these. Now the vocal brother consulted your ledger, slowly thumbing the pages, muttering as if he were reading phrases aloud, before finally he seemed to read: "And when the Preacher does pass this man Young will ascend to his place," but would allow none to see the text within. And many furious debates were held. And there were those who said your son "contained the blood of the revelation." And at the moment of the vote the silent brother stepped from the shadows, speaking in what many considered "the voice of a lion," and such was his booming voice that they believed your hand at work. And he said, "I am no Preacher, but I will be a president." Now some saw him grown into the shape of the creature of old, no more the bulbous beast of your later days, for now the horror was svelte, now hooves and horns and leathery wings, and many said they scented soot and brimstone upon the wind. So these priests voted in favor of his ascendance while his brother and your son received no votes.

III. And the spurned brother whispered to those who would listen: "I have known this fellow all my life—I tell you we cannot trust him." And in the hours to follow that brother was found headless by the river.

IV. And following his brother's death, the president called your wife to his side. "I have ever found you a compelling woman," the president told her, and now he touched her knee. Over his right shoulder the creature's eyes gleamed, and so she knew well that lurid look. Afterward, your wife went to your son, telling him to flee. "Only terrible times may follow," she said. He shook his head. "I will take what is mine," he said. And when your wife told him the president would come for him your son replied, "That may be so, but he does not understand what I have inside me." And now your son touched her hand, and he called Samuel and Samuel's wife to his side, and to them your son said, "Everything will be fine now. You will see."

And your wife left this land by horse alone. And all said she would return. And all were wrong.

And what of those who have said your wife returned in later days, her second husband with her, as the hour went into night, and the gesture of His hand went across the land?

I will tell you.

She arrived in the town of your death as the sky fled to black and the meteors trailed and lit all the land. How frail she seemed, leaning on her walking stick, and how slow she now moved while her husband waited in the carriage.

How slowly she lowered herself to the dust before your stone. And she touched the stone's smoothness, lit crimson and orange by the light behind.

And she whispered to the dirt, "Do you recognize an old woman?" and she said, "Are you below me? Have you watched me the days of my life?" and she said, "If I opened the ground would I find you?" and she pressed her ears to the earth, and she heard not your struggle, and she felt not the pulse of your life returned. And when she said, "If I went to the top of that mountain—" she gestured to the black mountain on the horizon. And now it was gone.

V. And you moldered in your box while the president sent a cherry-cheeked youth to the militia camps, proclaiming they were fleeing the land in peace. Now many piled their wagons with chairs and lamps and books and framed portraits and shelves and dried beans and oats and casks of water. And now this mass of followers, who prayed to the ghost and memory of their Preacher each night, drifted ever westward, first into the dying of the trees and the fading of the grasses, and then into the blackening skylines. And when they passed farmers who knew your preaching the farmers and their families hissed and threw sod. And when they continued beyond the regions in which you were known now the farmers and their wives brought pies and loaves of bread, jars of black and red wild berry preserves. And then the coming rains blurred the horizon and your people, bent against the winds, and after the lashing rains they huddled in the mud and the slop. And priests embraced wives, and children bound up with siblings and their young beloveds, chattering and numb for the anguish and the chill. And on they trudged, ever westward, the line of wagons extending miles. And when the snows massed many became feverish and they collapsed, hallucinating, shivering in the drifts, and soon these bodies were shrouded with snow, made anonymous beneath the mound, gone into nameless bone in the spring, become one with a thousand species of skulls, ever moldering and threaded through by much the same wild flowers. Still the president pressed them onward—this president driven by what some feared was madness, warmed through by the blast furnace of the creature's soul. And wagons caught in the drifts, and dresses caught in the wheels, and now wives were crushed beneath the weight of their possessions. And many fell with blackened feet and hands, coughing blood, starving and caved in, and so these people were crushed beneath the wheels of oncoming wagons, the hooves of oxen, the slow, mindless trudge of their fellow pilgrims.

VI. And they found many husks of great animals, some frozen in the midst of decay. And within these animals were discovered many birds and creatures of plunder, their mouths stuffed full of meat. And many dead creatures, birds and bison and coyotes, populated the snow, gazing outward with expressions fixed and doomed.

And they erected tents and fires, if the winds and snows allowed, or they slouched against the wagons, covered over with skins, waking buried and impossibly warm and stifled. And they recollected your sayings, your visions, your teachings, your humor, your kindnesses, and they wept until the president said, "He sleeps no more in the dust, for I have seen our Preacher on the mountain, overfilled with life, for there everything stands shining." And none noticed your son left the camp during these speeches. Gone until the light of camps seemed frail and distant.

VII. Through this time your son remained with Samuel and Samuel's lone wife. He had not taken a second wife, and he never would. Now nights Samuel's wife spoke only in whispers and Samuel spoke to her in rough, abrupt commands, in loud voices, while writing out the language he truly meant to express: "*I do not trust the president.*" And his wife nodded: "*I know.*" Now they burned the paper and obliterated the ash. Your son, smiling before them in the firelight, said, "It will work out. You will see, Papa and Mother."

And when a wild dog, snarling and emaciated and wild eyed, ventured from the dark, Samuel raised his rifle but your son said no. And the dog smelled your son's palm and the dog sat with immaculate posture as your son scratched behind its ears. "You will see," said your son. "We have nothing to fear."

VIII. And when your son fell feverish Samuel's wife wiped his brow and covered him in furs as he rode in the back of their wagon. There your son, pale and barely bearded, something like a man and yet a child always to the citizens of your church, lay chattering and unable to move, his lips cracked and bloody. And carrion birds observed from wagon tops, and many wolves slunk in the outer dark, their yellow eyes fixed upon your son. Many priests too gathered about your son, praying to the Almighty for deliverance. And Samuel and Samuel's wife stood always with your son. And Samuel placed hands upon the boy. And when he touched the dead icy skin he jerked away. And he wept, and when he tried to stop he could not. Now his wife held him, and so it was she who went to the president, asking him to lay hands upon your son. He refused. "I am no prophet. I am no healer," he said. "His father was a healer." And a cry went up until finally the president relented. And now your son's lids opened. "I know you are a liar," the boy said. "I am to lead this church." And only the president heard your son. And then the boy fell silent and his lids closed. And the president announced to all, "It is a tragedy, but our Prophet's son has gone home to his fathers." And Samuel's wife said, "I heard my son speak!" And the president said, "Only the rustling of the wind, I assure you."

And many fell to weeping. And birds beat their wings with fury, blackening the sky with their flight, and the wolves and coyotes cried in chorus like deranged trumpets. And no man would take up arms against these animals, no matter the president's commands, for some said your hand guided the beasts, while others said, "The citizens of the forest did ever favor that child." So they carried your son into the nearby forest, as it began to snow, laying him beneath the shelter of pines, the flakes ever descending and covering. And before the president departed, your son opened his eyes. "He will know what you have done," the boy gasped. And his eyes blazed: "I have seen Him, crimson in the fire of the light, and He will come for you, gnashing." And the president soothed, "Sleep now. This is all a dream." And so the president left.

And the flakes that fell upon your son melted. And the birds and dogs that came to pick at his body sniffed and backed away. From a distance they moaned and whimpered. And like strange planets in orbit, they circled him, fixed by some relation unknown to all, although the theories have been many.

IX. And when Samuel and his wife now woke in the night, they believed the creature had come, breathing brimstone, for they had dreamed the monster's howl, echoing with the voice of your son, and a piercing light, the beauty and the horror of the creature. And while all else slept, Samuel and his wife went to your son's body, his figure surrounded by every manner of beast. All animals in mutual silence gazed unto your son's uncovered body. His body was unmoving, and his body did not breathe, and when they spoke to the body the body did not speak back, but Samuel and his wife gathered your son, loose and heavy, in their arms anyway. At their wagon they covered him with blankets and skins. And they told no one—not the president, and not any of the priests or the many wives. And so they journeyed with the body of your boy, bundled and at rest. And none questioned why so many birds trailed in the heavens, and none wondered why so many wild dogs kept pace along the distance.

X. And when a shape of darkness passed overhead the president insisted, "It is His mighty creature watching over us." And he said, "You see how it favors me?" And none would deny this insight.

XI. And they continued. And those families who would wait until the spring months to flee would pass over the skeletons and ragged clothing and rotting wheels and oxen ribs and thinly dug graves of those who passed before. And they would cross themselves. And they would weep. And they would say the name of the Almighty. And they would say your name.

And they continued no matter how many died on the trail. And they continued no matter the apparent aimlessness of their journey. No matter if the structure of a ridge seemed familiar, and no matter if a pile of skulls seemed to mark the grave of priests, none mutinied and none turned back. And no matter how far they traveled the black mountain remained on the horizon.

And after the areas of snows came piñon buckled with cones and the blue and purple bursting of wild flowers. And when natives came to trade the president swapped pots and pans for comely squaws, joking to his closest advisors, "There's nothing these heathen girls won't do." And as the squaws became ever more numerous the president said, "I think I'll see how many I can have at one time." His many squaws gathered into his tent, the noises and motions of their crowded play, the giggling and the president's hee-hawing laughter, while the other wives looked at one another in silence.

And they passed by rock formations illustrated with the pictographs of forgotten peoples. And they passed by the husks of many dead bison. And they passed by carrion birds hunched on rocks and swirling overhead. And some said they saw the shadows of natives on the sandstone hillsides, and some said these were mirages or apparitions. And some said the creature walked amongst them for the hoofprints stamped in the mud and the brimstone breeze that always blew. And now they traveled always under the throbbing of the sun, and the heat pressed deeply into their brains.

And when they came to a valley laden with flowers and mountains everywhere on the horizon, the president motioned for the pilgrims to stop. And now he went into the prairie, and at the edge of the grasses he found a body of water, and he fell to his knees. Geese took flight at his presence, and now his voice was heard dimly on the wind, speaking in a voice of rapture. Finally he returned, his knees heavy with fresh mud and his hair entirely white. "We will call this place Deseret," he said, "for we have found our land of plenty."

XII. And all knew His hand had prepared for their arrival, for here they found houses constructed of wood and brick, and doors of wood, and windows of glass. And here they found streets of brick and stone. And here they found buildings for shops. And they found buildings for restaurants and hotels and tithing houses. And when counted there were enough houses for all the families, and houses enough for many of the families of those yet to come.

And within these houses they found no rugs, or furniture, or books, or shelves, or food, or artwork, or portraits. They found only the absence of life, and they found the fulfillment of life that is the dust, everywhere fallen and covering. And when they asked whom these houses belonged to the president said, "They belong to us," and when they asked, "Whom did these houses belong to?" then the president said, "They belonged to the original peoples," and when none believed these houses were a millennia old the president shrugged his shoulders and said, "But it is so."

And all called this land Deseret, which means not "paradise" but "honeybee." And all recognized this land from your book, although none could recall the page numbers where the land was in this way described.

XIII. And the president moved his wives and possessions into the largest house on the highest hill. This house, hued in blackness, as if the pillars were carved from obsidian and the windows smote with soot. And this house seemed to vibrate with heat. And who did not see the creature, vast and dripping pitch, perched upon the roof? And who did not know this swollen monster, filling the rooms with its corpulence? And who did not see the president conversing with this beast, the flicker of its horrid tail, the pulsing of its reddened eyes? And what man would not call it just and true that his president lived within the largest home and was ever in conversation with the most terrible creature of God?

XIV. And all moved their families and possessions into these ancient houses. And so too did Samuel and his wife. And they moved your son into their home and on a table they laid him, covered with blankets and furs, while the ceiling sighed under the burden of squirrels and birds. There your son lay, not breathing or moving or bulging with gas or decaying. And when they pulled aside the blanket he seemed as always. And when they whispered to him there came no reply. And when they read to him from your book they knew only the absence of his prayer. And in the stillness of his hands, his breast, they knew the love of their daughter. They knew the way the world had been long before any had known of this land. They knew that love once blossomed is doomed to fall into the absence of sound and life. They knew only the voice of their weeping, the agony of their sobs. They knew when they kissed his brow nevermore would the young man beneath kiss them back. And when they clasped his hands they knew only the absence of give in them. And when they brushed his brow they knew only the coldness beneath.

XV. Soon after the establishment of Deseret, five native men with red-painted faces and buzzard feather plumes led two ragged native boys into what was called the town square. The boys were bleeding and bruised and bound at the wrists, and the native leader indicated they were the sole survivors of a rival tribe he had slaughtered. Now they were his gift unto your people as a "token of friendship." A cry went up amongst the pilgrims, for a man's life is no gift unto another man. And so now the chief drew a red line across the throat of the taller of the two boys, no peep from him as his head dropped, and his knees, and his body through his knees. And the women shrieked and the men reached for their pistols and Samuel cried from the throng, "I will take the child." So this solution was agreed upon, but the boy pulled away when Samuel reached for him. And the boy struggled against the rope, gritting his teeth until blood speckled his lips. His eyes bulged and his tendons stood out and his shoulders sagged and his eyes teared, and he continued, the red raw of his hands, and the sobs choking his throat. When finally they reached Samuel's house, the child fled into the depths, his silent native scamper. They found him in none of the closets, or about the yard, or in any of the bedrooms, or beneath any of the beds, and finally they found the smudged imprints of his feet. Soon they found the boy cowering on his haunches beneath the table your son lay upon.

There he remained, cowering, refusing to emerge for his food, and so Samuel's wife slid the plate into the dark. And slowly the child emerged. And now he trailed Samuel's wife as she performed her tasks. When Samuel was certain no outsider would hear he would call his wife the name she was born with, and so the child learned to mimic this sound. And the boy took slow to his bathing, refusing to enter the tub or even touch the heated water. And he bristled at the trimming of his locks, but he showed a good nature and spoke openly in his tongue when Samuel spoke to him. At night Samuel read to him, his fingers tracing the lines, and the boy's eyes followed along. And when Samuel opened a dry goods shop near the town square now the boy followed at his side, cowering behind barrels of dried beans when customers entered, his black eyes peering. And when they were again alone Samuel opened his arms, saying one of his many names for the boy, and the child ran to him, and in the young boy's heat, his scrawny embrace, Samuel remembered much of the pain come to pass. And when they returned home every manner of fowl and cat and squirrel blanketed the roof with fur and feathers and silent, watching eyes. And to these the boy pointed and Samuel said, "Yes, my lad. So many creatures come to see your brother."

XVI. Soon by presidential commandment, Samuel and his native boy led the president and a delegation of a few into the wilderness depths unbroken by light and illuminated by the eyes of wolves alone. The boy was leashed by the president's command, and so reluctantly he went, until they found the flickering of fires. There natives crouched before thatched lodges and buckskin tents. And here they existed in what they called "peace," although they held no industry of their own but the raiding and pillaging of other peoples, and in this way they obtained horses, tin pots, knives, and rifles.

And the chief was a man of some width and girth, and to him the president made a gift of your book, and he lectured on how the natives and their savage ways fit into your philosophy, for indeed "when your savage nations have converted this world will then heave its final breath."

And leather trunks and burlap sacks loaded with plates and pots and candles and utensils were lugged by pilgrim men, and placed at the chief's feet while he gnawed roasted venison. The gloomy dark of his thatched ceiling, the stink of the meat and the fire smoke, and all the dim-lit faces surrounding, crouched on their animal hides and gazing outward at the president and his fellows. And the chief and his cabinet and his priests wore bird masks and the masks of jackals and the masks of monsters unknown. Now the chief spoke with his advisors, with his priests, and they praised the greatness and novelty of the gifts. That night many ducks and geese and antelope and deer and wild dogs were roasted over this fire, and all feasted on the meat and grease and roasted bones, until the faces of the president and his men were fat slick and smiling. In the next days the president led this chief into the chill waters of the nearest river, and there baptized the old pagan in the name of the Almighty.

And the president called the natives "delightful." And he enjoyed patting the chief upon his head, and they talked often of the "Great Father to the east" neither trusted, the one they would "someday eliminate."

XVII. And while the men fed, Samuel's native boy indicated the mountains. And had they allowed him to lead them there, they would have followed ancient winding paths into the dripping mouths of caves, piled over with mossy boulders, while within lay the bodies of the pale-skinned Admiral and his many pale-skinned advisors, and the various men of his court. This man had come from the sea and subjugated much of the land to his indomitable will, and at the hour of his death he commanded all to share in his end. Had the president ordered those caves opened they would have found untold depths, and had they lit torches and gone into those corridors, had they ducked for the dripping of stalactites, had they ventured through the dank and poisonous oxygen, they would have found chambers upon chambers crowded with the bones of men, their golden armor and helmets, their swords and rifles, the rot of their plumes, boots, trousers. And before the counselors and supplicants of the Admiral, the bodies of his jesters, their bronzed bells, their leather motley, and the bodies of their wives, children in their arms, those who died first. And trailing the floors and the walls, the long browned scrawls of fingers clawed raw, ripping at the boulders and the floors, and then their own throats, and then the throats of the fellow nearest, and then chewing at the dead and decaying meat of the fellow nearest. And perhaps one man took a rock from the floor and hefted this into the bare skull of the man next to him, devouring in his last moments this fellow he had known long years and slept by and gone to war with, and then that man, fattened and full, would slowly continue forth into the inevitable. And within the farthest chambers they would have found upon some ancient table the golden-armored body of the Admiral himself, a man become mere grinning bone and dust. These men, who clamored for gold, who clamored for gods, come from lands unknown and forced by native torch and by native spear to their demise. And finally the president stooped to the jabbering boy, saying, "Yes, yes, we have known mountains in our time too." And to Samuel the president said, "I have heard enough of his braying."

XVIII. And the president married the chief's youngest and comeliest daughter, she with the averted eyes and bashful finger to her pink lip. The president named her "Rose Blossom" and gave her the room closest to his chambers. Many nights now he went to her, lingering well beyond the dawn, her youthful hand resting in the tufts of his chest, what he called "the lion's mane."

XIX. So went the days of prosperity and grace. Now the president's wives held many balls within their mansion. And the pilgrims wore the common clothing of their own manufacture in place of the outfits of former greatness, those tuxedos and silk gowns, lost in the course of their many nighttime rides, in trunks fallen and moth eaten and burned. And the earth ran thick and red with the blood of many calves and lambs and chickens and geese and deer and antelope, so the banquet tables could heap with flesh. And the president increased in girth until his belts no longer fit and his shirt buttons snapped, for each night he attended a new ball, or stopped at a pilgrim's home, commanding "the slaughter of your best calf and lamb" and supping mightily upon these, doused always with the richest gravies.

And men such as Samuel amassed small fortunes, and farmers and orchards and livestock flourished. And travelers and wagon trains here refreshed their goods, for no other city for a thousand miles had achieved such wealth. And the president was heard to say, "Prosperity is earned only through the firmness of the Father," and he commanded his angels to ransack houses for hints of intransigence or wavering allegiance. Letters were steamed open and read, and desk drawers rifled through, and spies were planted within closets and under beds. And those who suggested the president had not the touch of the divine, or who doubted your word, or who questioned the president when he arrived at their doorstep with his carriage and said their "daughter" or their "sister" or their "comeliest wife" was to become his wife, or become the wife of one of his supporters, disappeared from their beds, or were found in the fields and in the prairies, slit through the neck, or shot through the skull, or filled with arrows.

XX. Evenings now Samuel slid discontented notes across the dinner table—"*We should flee*" and "*He cannot be trusted.*" So his wife read them and nodded. He burned these twice over and smeared the ash beneath his bootheel. And always the cats and birds and squirrels, unwavering in their fixation, ever silent and nestled upon the roof and bulging within the trees, while your son remained shrouded within an oak chest, propped open during most days and closed whenever visitors neared.

XXI. Finally then the president visited Samuel's house without warning or notice, his carriage of gold festooned with ribbons red and blue. Once inside he spoke of the animal stink and the animals, strange in their vigilance. And to Samuel he said, "You know, I bet a good fire would do wonders with those types. Always does." And he called Samuel's home "most modest," while detecting what he called "a certain rot—does some creature perhaps lie dead beneath your floors?" Now he regarded the chest where your son was, touching his brow as if light-headed, and he said nothing. At the table with bib unfurled, he devoured a whole chicken, rich sauce dripping, sucking his grease-slick fingers. And his angels remained in the shadows, arms crossed, their eyes fixed upon Samuel. And the native boy locked himself within the darkness of the pantry, weeping and trembling whenever the president spoke or belched. And when the president finished his feast he regarded Samuel's wife and he said, "Such a fine meal." And Samuel's wife blushed. And Samuel said, "Yes, my wife is a marvelous cook," and the president sucked on another finger, and then a loud pop, and then he sucked another, his gaze fixed ever upon her while he said, "Such a cook within my home would please me." And he said, "And to have such a wife within my bed." And Samuel's eyes bulged. And he tried to speak but no sound came. Now the president rose and gestured for Samuel's wife to follow. And by this he meant for her to leave her home without packing or saying a word. And when she seemed not to leave of her own accord the president wrenched his hand in her hair: "You will see how a lion may roar." And when she only struggled

and wept the president continued: "I can make this man disappear as if he never happened—would that make this easier?"
Only now did she move, disappearing into the shadow of the
president's girth, and throughout these motions Samuel did not
look above his hands, nor did he speak, nor did he shift, until
the door closed and the boot steps faded down the walk. Now
Samuel gulped for air, while the angels remained with arms
crossed and weapons ready. They would kill him if he spoke.
Surely he had known these men for many years, risen from the
same dust, in the same yard, but he could not recall them. And
in the moments after the president and his new bride left, the
only sounds heard were the sounds of cats yowling and squirrels scratching and birds picking at the roof.

XXII. Each day all filed into the temple, and there the
president alone stood at the fore, preaching, "I
wish to save life and have no desire to destroy life," and "I do
not have one single feeling against any man or woman on earth,"
and "Love the Almighty. Love each other," and "A woman is the
glory of man, but she was not made to be worshipped by him,"
and "The man who abuses or brings dishonor upon the female
sex is a fool and does not know that his mother and sisters are
women," and he said, "Absolute tyranny never can produce hap-
piness," and "I would rather have the Almighty as my friend,
and all the world enemies, than be a friend with the world and
have the Almighty as my enemy." And Samuel watched from
the middle pew and he sang, and the native child sang, and
their hearts were filled with what they called "glory." And when
the boy saw Samuel's wife with the president's other wives
he scampered to her, and Samuel's once wife was made to
push the boy away—the boy's arms at her waist, and the president's new wife struggling to not cry. "Blessed are the children,"
said the president from his pulpit, to the laughter of all. "Even
this one."

XXIII. Now some families received permission to return to the trail. There they would exhume their dead, so those bones too would know the land of Deseret. They set out in carriages, entire families in tow, and along the trail they found only opened graves and bones scattered. And where they had left the thinly buried bodies of their lost loved ones marked with stones, now they found skulls cast about the prairies, exploded with purple flowers and thistles. Now those families wept in ways forbidden all those months. All bones now dealt into a deeper grave, the bones of animals mixed with the bones of man. And who could not wonder if at the moment of the resurrection these beloved would walk again the earth as confusions of nature, their skulls the skulls of wild dogs and their faces deformed with monstrous horns, while the wings of carrion birds protrude their backs. And over the fresh soil mounds the living read prayers from the pages of your book, and they sang from the hymnal of your wife's construction.

When the last words fled their lips, they shut their eyes and shielded their brows for the prairie winds gusting, and some families returned to their homes, and some fled back eastward. And for those who fled, the president summoned his angels, those riders lashing the range, their snorting horses, the bulging eyes and foam, until such a moment when the dust of the fleeing travelers bloomed on the horizon, and soon then bullets seared into the wives and children, while the husbands and fathers were bound with rope and made to see the blood leaking into the earth, the brains rolled with prairie dust. Finally the fathers were pressed to the dirt and axes dealt through their necks. These new dead too remained until such a time when weather, or animal, or insect, consumed the flesh, and cast the bones hither and thither.

XXIV. And when one of Samuel's neighbors suggested he should "manufacture some relatives," Samuel shook his head in a vague, wary way. "She will

return, eventually," he said. The neighbor looked at Samuel
blankly and now the boy said her name. Samuel's voice broke:
"I can't leave her, you see." Finally the neighbor indicated the
black mansion, how it shimmered and vibrated on the hillside.
"What if—" he began. "Forgive me, Brother Samuel, but what
if she likes it there?" Now Samuel returned indoors, the boy
scampering behind him, and then the door closed.

XXV. No matter, soon the president forbade any travel in or out of town, and instead he held services for the souls of all those who perished on the trail, calling the soil where their remains moldered "as good as consecrated." And his angels were posted on every street corner. Their silence, their shifting eyes, the dark suspicions they housed toward all.

And the president sent his angels to the homes of every male over the age of ten and beneath the age of forty, commanding them to prepare for the coming of a great many enemies into their midst. And he sent many of these men to the native chief's camps. How many tents burned and warriors shot through the skulls, necks, chests, grasping wounds and spitting blood, and yet continuing to fight while they drained into the soil, while they sloshed around. And how many women were shot through the skulls or slit across the throats. And how many infant children were bashed with rocks or stomped into oblivion. And how wretched was the sky, black with smoke, the black of tents and bodies burning, while horses thrashed and stampeded the mountains, and wild dogs watched from the forest, ravenous.

And when his squaw wives protested his butchery the president thrashed them with coils of rope until they fell, weary and rope reddened. And when they refused him in the hour of his longing he bound them with rope and cord, and now they were made to love him again. How he told his fellows the next day, over meals of goose and suckling pig, "These young squaws do call out," and "They resist at first, but once they get a taste they reveal their true natures, as lusty as any raised by whores." And all laughed, agreeing that a woman may feign reluctance or indifference, but the application of force will ever achieve the return of desire.

And how swollen was the night with the sounds of coyotes and wild dogs and hyenas and jackals, howling at the feast of a thousand bloated natives. And when the wind gusted now the waft of the decay. And carrion birds ever circled. And when the creatures at their feast bellowed, their throats choked with rot, now children in their beds woke and could no more sleep for their trembling. Fathers with rifles readied scanned the forest dark for yellow eyes, and women stood in the kitchens, or in the pantries, or over washtubs and boards, listening to the horrors without number. They could build a thousand temples over those graves, but never would those sounds end.

XXVI. And Samuel lay awake beneath the hundred, hundred squirrels and birds upon his roof, while the eyes of the wolves and the coyotes speckled his yard in the dark. And the native child slept on the chest except when Samuel peered within, and there your son, ever as before. And when they left for work and when they returned at night, the animals watched and waited. That never familiar sight. The anxiety always, and to see them anew the child's chest pulsed and his breathing rasped and Samuel held the back of his head, the soft black hair, the warmth of the skull, and he said, "Yes, I know." Ever the endless rows of black eyes and yellow beaks, wings and claws. And then the day they returned to find the kitchen window punched out and feathers and fur and blood trailing into the house. There a red fox asleep upon the chest, and then the beast awoke, snarling, and scampered past Samuel through the open door, blood trailing.

And as the hours passed the animals gathered in ever greater numbers, the sun gone absent, the windows blotted black but for the glow of their eyes. And so the air within the house was pungent with their feces and blood and fur. And now wild dog sat haunch to haunch with wild cat and wild bird. And more arrived from fields of dead natives, their bellies inflated with the raw meat of the murdered, bloodied beaks and maws and smeared red muzzles. They massed in the yard, rows upon rows of eyes and snouts, and gazed through the windows or into the walls, as if they perceived somehow the boy in the shadows and Samuel in his chair and the son of the man you were within the chest.

And then one dawn Samuel woke into a terrible vacuum, for no animal chirped, or yowled, or howled, or moaned, or snarled.

And this day the native child refused to leave the house. And when Samuel pulled him the boy shivered and wept, and when Samuel carried him the boy was sick upon himself. And finally the boy let out such an awful wail that Samuel left the room, and in the next room Samuel covered his ears for the horrid cry his child made and the terrible stillness of the animals everywhere.

XXVII. And those animals stirred not when armed riders stormed the road, nor when carriages stuffed with militia approached, nor at the firing of rifles into the sky, into their mass, nor at the plummet of their fellows, faces fixed in death grins, bloody fractured incisors, nor when these militia with rifles and pistols at the ready moved through their throngs, over the bodies already heavy with flies and ants, nor when these men rapped at the door, nor when they shouted Samuel's name, nor when they jolted the butts of their rifles into the door, nor when the door finally swung open. Samuel there with glazed expression, hair wild and whiskers long and unkempt. He spoke only in low moans, a gasp, and then, "What?" And those militiamen said, "Get your shovel. There has been a massacre."

Samuel went to find the boy and he found only trembling and screams. The boy somehow lost in the shadows. And Samuel wept. And finally he departed.

And the militia: their carriages, their horses, and Samuel gathered his horse from the barn. The horse would not move.

It would not stop gazing at the house. How he lashed this beast, the blood glistening across the flank, before he could lead it through the throng of a thousand animals. And all his soul longed to remain, to hold that boy in his terror. But he did not.

And the farther Samuel rode the less reluctant his horse. And deeper into the desert, the lizards and rabbits scurrying, the misshapen birds circling, until now the clouds of dust and the canvas of a hundred wagons, the milling of men, their rifles, and beyond them the figures of gentile men and women and children, in postures of surrender, the silent weeping of the children, the shushing of their mothers. And when Samuel neared they rode to him, calling out, "Where's your gun?" and Samuel said, "I don't need a gun to bury bodies." They called him now a "fool" and an "imbecile." They spat onto the dirt, and they told him to return home to the rest of the milksops. And the stark expression of gentile men and women and children led into wagons, and now gunshots and screams following on the wind as Samuel returned along the plains. The spray of the blood and brains against the canvas, and the flight of women and children and men into the dirt, dispersing across the prairie while men stalked with rifles, the women flowering with blood and the second shot into their skulls, and a third, the children clubbed with rifles butts, and once they fell, bloody and limp, then they too were shot through the skull, while distorted birds circled, and hyenas and jackals peered over the rocks—soon now, this their kingdom. And the gentile men who fought back were beaten to the ground and kicked in the bellies and bludgeoned with rifles, and then shot through the skulls. And when children hid behind rocks they were found and they were shot through the eyes, or they were led quivering and weeping into carriages to be "redeemed." Soon the blood pour. And when women scampered behind trees or over the hills they were caught and dragged down by their hair and slit across the throat, or fucked screaming and then murdered with rocks punched into their faces. And when men scampered they were shot in the backs and fell blossoming blood and then set upon by two or three men at a time with knives and rifles, hacking and firing and cursing and spitting. Blood and flies and mounded dead, this city of murder. And when all were dead save a few children, now the pockets of the dead were rifled through and jewelry snapped off and pocketed, and so all the possessions reattributed to the living. And soon living women were seen in the streets, attired in the clothing and jewelry of dead gentile women. And what man would not wish to be known in the outfit of the gentile he stalked and shot, and bashed into bone and guts, and spat upon and stripped nude, and left for the flies and dogs and carrion birds to pick apart?

XXVIII. And Samuel returned home to the absence of animals. Now there remained only blood and feces and fur and loose teeth streaking his house. And the doors had been torn off their hinges. And the windows were burst in, the shards streaked with blood and clumped with fur. And paw prints scattered in blood and mud and feces. And feathers and tufts of fur drifted the hallways as if drifts of winter snow. And here the intolerable musk of gore and frenzy. And here the flies, constant and without number. And here the corpses of those animals killed in the rush were strewn throughout the rooms, half eaten and covered with flies.

And the native boy's head lay in the parlor, the eyes and cheeks and tongue eaten out. And what remained of his torso was slopped in the sitting room. And the half-eaten remains of a leg and an arm were in the yard. And the shroud that once wrapped your son was red with gore and strewn throughout the house. And the oak chest was torn to pieces. And no aspect of your son remained, save his footprints, stamped in blood upon the floors and out the door.

In Samuel's familiar chair rested already the half-eaten carcass of a small dog and one of the native child's limbs, so instead he went to the dining table, and there he rest his elbows, and now his brow, upon the blood- and feather-filthy surface. And from afar came the sounds of gunshots yet echoing, or perhaps the throbbing in his ears, and then only the silence of the world. And how deafening now the absence of the animals, how riotous the buzzing of flies.

XXIX.

And perhaps in a dream and perhaps in the night hours, Samuel rose from his sleep. Through the mist of the yard he went, along the path of the blood tracks, and here in hordes of hundreds lay the dead, the serene and blood-stiffened faces of birds and rabbits and wild dogs. This trail of dead now Samuel followed. And he followed them into the forests and he followed them out of the forests. And he followed them along the stretches of vast open land, the dead land of the deserts, the gray emptiness of rocks and cacti and ruin.

And he followed them through the misted field. And he followed them across the desert stretches of skull and rib and femur.

And he followed them to the moment when the black mountain loomed and seethed on the horizon. And he followed them through the forests of suicides, the swinging bloat. And he followed them to the base of the black mountain. Here the rocks and dust and outcroppings of weeds, vibrating. Here the carrion birds circling overhead seemed to shrivel within the hum. Here your son's blood tracks continued, and the clumps of fur, and the feathers, yes, ever up the mountain they went.

And so Samuel climbed. His fingers raw and warped and his arms numb and his throat constricted. And he continued through the swirling cloud and the noxious shimmering atmosphere. In the vast night, stars flickered and strange fires burst and smoldered and trailed the skies. And for a time all seemed lit below.

And here the skeleton of a man, fallen against the black stone. And here the skull. And here another man's rotten costume, the canvas clothes and no bones within, perhaps scorched to dust, perhaps blown away. And here an obsidian rock rubbed crimson. And here another stone bore the name of a man, or perhaps a message, carved into it, the lettering long obscured and distorted by time.

And Samuel continued beyond the moment of sense, through the ways of endurance, until he reached the peak. And here he found the ground leveled out. He seemed to sway in the gusting and swirling winds, the wrapping mists. And at the outer edge of the peak was a copper telescope. And at the opposite edge stood a cabin painted black. And the windows were of glass and shining, though no light shone from within.

And the building did not shift or seethe or vibrate. And there was no sound from within. And no man came to the door, but there was a door, and it had a knob, and the knob was the color of night.

And in the moment he waited before this cabin, Samuel witnessed the scenes and movements of all he had ever known. And then Samuel opened the door, and he went inside.

EPILOGUE
THE ANCIENT BEAST

WHEN THEIR DAYS TRAMPING THE WILDS PROVED WITHOUT MERIT
they returned to the beaches. Their ship sunk in the bay as if eviscerated by some ancient and terrible beast. And in the open sun, new
plants and animals grew in place of the charred remains of the old.
And they found neither bone nor char nor any other evidence that
human life once walked these shores, until they found the rusted
anchor of some ship perhaps moored and rotted into nothingness a
thousand years prior embedded in the sands. And a many-colored
bird landed on the anchor's edge, reptilian eyes bulging, and the bird
spoke the name of the chief they had murdered. And the bird took
flight when they lifted their muskets to fire, the alien shrill of its
voice cackling as it fled.

And they constructed a shanty of banana fronds for the Admiral
to sleep beneath, while the crew slumbered under the stars, dreaming of the houses they would build on this beach, houses in the style
and fashion of those owned by merchants they had known in their
youths. And in the dawn they chopped timber, and with their bare
hands they dug foundations, and here in the soil lay the scattered
skulls and bones of men and the armor of these men, their rusted
helmets and breastplates. How the crew crouched and gazed into
the empty sockets of some long-ago man. The Admiral ordered them
thrown into a pyre. When the fire perished and bones and armor yet
protruded the ash, the Admiral ordered a yet greater fire constructed.
And the terrible immensity of this new flame, the eyebrows and arm
hairs of the crew curling into white ash, and the black smoke, and
the crackling and snapping into oblivion of what lay beneath.

In the days to follow they raised up many structures, the shadows of the beams falling in the shapes of bones. And they were no more the men they had been, for now their eyes blazed red and black, now they were hued ebony and their hair was wild, rife with lice and fleas.

Now the outline of a city raised, birds perched atop the beams, silhouetted and screaming, while lizards crouched and hissed in doorways. And in their hours of labor, when one man spoke to the next he did so in a language of his own construction and the other fellow answered back in guttural tones. And when one man looked into the black and cavernous eyes of the next he knew no more the soul of the fellow who watched from within. When a man hungered he ventured into the wild with his sword, and there he murdered a monkey while its fellows danced and beat their paws against a tree. And these the men skinned and wrapped in banana leaves and roasted over coals. They brought steaming handfuls of flesh to the Admiral, who now wore only monkey skins fashioned into the robe of a holy man. Through the hours of the day he muttered to the mountain, pressed his brow to the earth, and in so doing he said the name of the Almighty.

And when a man fell to fever or when a man in his sorrow attempted self-slaughter or a man crazed for want of a woman coupled with another man, he was shackled and led to the Admiral, who laid hands upon him. And the Admiral said, "We could not find Paradise for we carry it within," and he said, "We must forsake the inelegance of the flesh, for only then will we understand peace."

And he commanded they pray through all hours of the day. And he commanded they make burnt offerings: the monkeys they slit open and roasted upon the cinders, the smoke of cooked monkey wafted toward the mountain with banana fronds.

And the Admiral thrashed in his sleep, and it was said he knew the names of the dead upon his lips. And it was said he knew the dead atop the mountain, watching him and gnashing. Someday they would come for him. They stood in the shadow of a monstrous creature, beneath the black wings of this beast, the red eyes of fire, and now around them the yellow teeth.

When he woke he wrote on the sands of the beach a misshapen and impossible language, an alphabet of images only, of mutilations and many-headed beasts, and within this transcription the Admiral believed he detected "the end of time."

When the sky filled with the light of a dozen fireballs, staining the night's blackness with trails of yellow and red, the Admiral stood in the tatters of his robe, calling out in a voice hoarse and hollow, "Hosanna, hosanna." And he held out his arms as if in wait, as if the creature would swoop from the burning night and take now the Admiral into its belly. And his men watched in horror, and they watched in awe. They watched with hands clasping swords.

When at dawn something immense moaned in the bay the Admiral said, "He waketh from his slumber," and when the dark seemed lit with the yellow of the eyes of a grand and impossible beast the Admiral said, "He disapproves of our worship." So the Admiral commanded each man to bathe in the salt water, to light a fire upon the shore, to offer into the flame some minuscule animal, to stamp his brow to the ash and mud. So they did. Now the men slowly disappeared from the shore. No screams were heard. No violence seen. Their bodies simply washed ashore some hours later, torn at the throat and their chest cavities crawling with crabs. The remaining men peered into the blackness of the bay: the dim shadows of fish, weeds tangled in the murk, and then darkness, mystery, nothingness. And when a thousand, thousand stars melted across the blackness, these men in their simple experience understood the lights merely hinted at the depth of the universe. And in this way those men understood the darkness of the bay scarcely hinted at the horrors below. To these few the Admiral lectured: "We struggle futilely when we believe we move with ease." He said, "We grope in a darkness we believe to be a world well lit."

And when only one crew member remained the Admiral summoned him to his shanty. The Admiral in the rotten skins of his robe, his tangled and lice-filthy beard, the sacred hollows of his eyes. And now the man asked, "What howls in the night? What murders our number?" and the Admiral said, "It is our Father who sits on the mountain, for He lives in all things." The Admiral touched this man on the chest. "He was in the men we murdered," said the Admiral. The man nodded, and he contemplated, and finally he asked, "In the women as well?" And to this the Admiral returned only silence.

And in the night the man burned a lizard by the shore and he prayed to the Almighty upon the mountain. Soon the screams of this man were lost within the roaring of some awesome and eternal beast. And then the Admiral alone remained.

And when the Admiral fell he fell by some affliction long latent in the flesh. He fell feverish onto the floor of a house built for another man. He fell shivering. He fell saying the names of the natives crowding the peak of the mountain, milling and watching with dank, absent sockets. He fell in the shadow of the creature come before him, this towering apparition of teeth and wings, and flame and roaring, claws and sinew and blood, horror and eternity. He fell as the beast lifted aside the roof and opened its savage maw. And in the voice of every language it said the name of the man given by his father, and it said the name gifted unto the man by the Almighty upon His black mountain.

And the Admiral's name has not been uttered in all the years since.

ACKNOWLEDGMENTS

I MUST FIRST ACKNOWLEDGE THE EDITORS OF THE FOLLOWING PUB-lications, where portions of *The Revelator* previously appeared: *A-Minor*, the *Atticus Review*, *Everyday Genius*, *Newfound*, and *PANK*.

I must also thank Chris Backley, Steve Himmer, and Amber Sparks for commenting on early drafts of *The Revelator*. Thanks also go to Matt Bell, Blake Butler, Eugene Marten, Joshua Mohr, and Lidia Yuknavitch for their generous blurbs and Matt Kish for the beauti-ful cover and illustrations.

Further gratitude is owed to Kent D. Wolf for his hard work on behalf of this novel and to Chris Heiser and Olivia Smith for taking on the book.

And finally, and as always, to Karissa and Iris, for placing a light within the darkness.

ABOUT THE ARTIST

Matt Kish created the epic work *Moby-Dick in Pictures: One Drawing for Every Page* (Tin House) and is a self-taught artist and librarian. He lives in Ohio with his wife, their two frogs, and far too many books.